CANE IS

ABLE

I AM 7

ACKNOWLEDGEMENTS

I would like to thank the Holy Spirit for allowing me to see a glimpse of the work that He is performing in the world today. I also want to thank all of the people that God placed in my path to help me to accomplish the vision that He gave me for this book. Their contributions, along with the direction and provision of the Holy Spirit, have encouraged and sustained me as this book unfolded in my spirit.

God Bless and Come now Lord Jesus!

I am 7

SBN-13: 978-1461047575
ISBN-10: 1461047579

Cover Art and Design: Anthony Crisafulli and Lorenzo Pace

Twaddel Pubishing
Easton, PA

 **Twaddel**

INSPIRATIONAL SCRIPTURE

"Behold, I send you out as sheep in the midst of wolves.
Therefore be wise as serpents and harmless as doves."
Matthew 10:16 (KJV)

TABLE OF CONTENTS

CHAPTER 1

SHELIA AND ARMANI

Armani opened his laptop and looked at his watch with dread. It was exactly 6:00 p.m. and time to make "the call" to his wife. He picked up the phone and dialed the number. When Shelia answered, Armani in a slow and monotone voice said, "Hey, lady. How you doing?" Shelia excitedly replied, "Hi, Armani. How are you?!" Trying to maintain his professional voice, he replied, "I'm doing just fine…Look, Shelia…I will be late again tonight." Armani paused, distracted by "voices" that he could hear speaking in his head.

One voice in Armani's head spoke softly and quietly. A second voice was louder and more forceful. (The Still Small Voice in Armani's head said, "Armani, you know that's a lie. You are not working late." Loud Voice: "Look Mani, why you trippin!? It's just a little white lie. What's the harm? Besides, you are always working... inside your head.")

Shelia responded, sounding sad, and asked, "Armani, you are working late again?" Armani responded, trying to sound disappointed also, "Yeah. Mr. Peterson wants the Stockholders' Quarterly Report on his desk by 9:00 Monday morning. I have to finish it."

Distracted from his conversation with Shelia, Armani once again became aware of the opposing voices in his head. (Still Small Voice: "Armani, stop lying!" Loud

Voice: "Look Mani, you're the head of your house. Just because you've finished the report doesn't mean you can't go over it again inside your head, like you are doing now.") Armani responded to Shelia's inquiry, "I'm really not sure. Just say I will be home late...Yes, again! I really gotta go. I'll see you later tonight. Bye!"

Using the intercom, Armani buzzed his assistant. She answered, "Yes, Mr. Lewis?" Armani continued, "Carol, get Ms. Alvarez on the line for me please." "Yes sir. Right away, Mr. Lewis." As soon as Armani had gotten the instruction out, he and his conscience had another exchange. (Still Small Voice: "Armani, stop this. You're thinking of committing adultery again. You know you're wrong. You shouldn't do that to Shelia!" Loud Voice: "Look Mani, you're a good looking man, and besides you work hard. Now it's time to play hard. Look, dude, it's Friday. Variety is the spice of life!")

A few minutes later, Armani heard the intercom engage and Carol's voice saying, "Mr. Lewis." "Yes, Carol." "Ms. Alvarez is on line two." Armani replied, "Thank you." Armani picked up the telephone and said in a low, deep voice, "Heeeey, baby girl." Martina answered flirtatiously, "Heeey Papi! How you doing?" Armani replied slowly, "Beautiful …beautiful…so, are you ready for me tonight?" Martina enthusiastically replied, "You bet I am, Mani!"

Smiling and laughing softly, Armani said, "Well, you must be wearing that black, form fitting dress that I love so much. Girl, I'm not sure if I like it better on or off!" Martina replied, "Mani, you're so bad!" Armani, smiling, replied, "I can't help it. You bring that out of me!" Looking at his watch and realizing there was work that must be finished before he left the office, he said, "Alright then....I will see you at 8:00 p.m. SHARP!"

After putting the telephone receiver down, Armani leaned back in his spacious office chair and smiled. Then once again, his conscience popped up and injected thoughts that interfered with his fantasy. (Still Small Voice: "Armani, think about Shelia at home with your child." Loud Voice: "Look Mani, picture Martina in that dress, the way it shapes her ample breasts, the way it hits her hips just so, the way men watch her when she enters the room. Then remember how she makes you feel... like a MAN!")

Armani snapped back to reality, realizing that he needed to finalize some details on the Seligman file. He knew that the account was important and that it just could be his stepping stone to a promotion. Although Armani had only been with the Lawson Advertising Firm for four years, he had already made junior vice-executive. He considered it a monumental feat for a "brother" to land a position with a prestigious advertising firm such as Lawson. It was located in Alpharetta, Georgia, and dominated by white professionals.

Armani believed that, if asked, most of his colleagues would admit their true thoughts about the basis for his rise in the adverting arena. He believed that most of them attributed his success to people giving him special treatment because of his football prowess and reputation. Rather than to his ability to compete not only on the football field, but also in the white collar advertising arena.

The word around the office was that Armani was

the token black guy who got all the big accounts. Apparently, 'affirmative action' was alive and well in his office, where their prevailing sentiment. They said that, "If he had not played football for Tech, he would not have not been employed with the firm as the janitor." But he most certainly would not have risen to the level of an executive, let alone a junior vice-executive at Lawson.

The presumption of tokenism among his colleagues did not bother Armani. He was proud of his football accomplishments and of the fact that he had worked hard all those years, despite having played for "peanuts." He felt that if his football success had carried over into the professional arena and was bringing him success there, so be it. He thought it was about time the fruits of his football labor paid dividends so he was not bothered by negative comments that he heard about his good deal. Reflecting on his colleagues, he asked himself, "Aren't white boys are always using their families and connections to benefit themselves? How is that any different than my using whatever connections I have to get ahead?!"

Armani remembered the low point in his life after blowing out his knee in his senior year of college and how good it felt good to finally get his business degree and to start making touch downs in life. He also thought about how his mother would have been so proud of him, especially since she never went to college. He drifted back to reality and began focusing on completing the Seligman file. He said out loud, "It looks like this will work."
Armani pressed the intercom and his assistant replied, "Yes, Mr. Lewis?" Armani continued, "Carol, can you

come here, please?" "Yes sir, Mr. Lewis." As Carol entered, Armani watched her pensively. Carol was an older white lady with a slightly overweight frame. She was always very courteous towards him, but Armani believed that she did not really care for him and that her cordial and respectful attitude was just game.

Carol had been the assistant for Armani's predecessor. When Armani assumed the executive position he could have replaced her. However, he decided that it would be wiser to have her on his team and to keep her around to help him learn the ropes. After he had gotten an opportunity to learn the basics about the position and the company politics, and if the chemistry between him and Carol did not take hold, he could let her go then. However, the main reason that Armani did not fire Carol, was that he was not attracted to her. She was perfect: she would not be a distraction to him and he would be able to stay focused while he was at work.

Hurriedly, Carol rushed in. She was wearing a plain, dark blue dress and black pumps. Her hair was pulled back in a bun. Armani thought to himself, "Even on a good day, my mind would not wonder about doing this librarian." Armani shook himself and smiled. Even as he considered this, he became aware of the voices speaking in his head. (Still Small Voice: "You sure do think about sex a lot." Laughing, the Loud Voice responded with, "Dude, you're a man. That's what you are supposed to think about, that and food. Oh yeah, don't forget football!")

"Carol, the Seligman file is ready for your approval," Armani said, smiling. Carol replied, "Oh, Mr. Lewis. I never make major changes…just some minor ones to make sure things add up." "I know, Carol, I'm just teasing you, he flashed his smile, and said, I need you to make sure the extrapolations that I've made make sense and see if the tables are coherent, over time, with inflation, please." Carol responded, "Yes sir, Mr. Lewis. I don't want us to get burned like 'Has Ben-Franklin' did on the Fisher account."

Armani remembered hearing about the infamous Fisher account, it had gained a lot of attention because if the finance department had not caught certain projection errors, the firm could have lost 7 million dollars. Armani replied, "Yeah, I heard about that. Too bad that happened to Franklin." But Armani thought to himself, "Business is business. Franklin made the mistake of trusting his administrative assistant to make the final proof of his work. My name is on these documents and I'm not letting any assistant lead me down the path of destruction!"

Armani imagined himself as the office joke and did not like what he saw, so it motivated him to cover himself by checking all of his figures seven times before giving the report to Carol to proof. He was not going to be labeled, "Has Ben-Franklin" like his predecessor.

Looking at the assortment of files she was handed, Carol said, "Will that be all, Mr. Lewis?" "That will be all, Ms. Caldwell," Armani replied. Though he was not really fond of Carol, he exchanged pleasantries with her for two reasons. First, he knew that he relied on her to get his job done. Second, he was heeding the advice that his Mother had repeatedly given him: "Boy, you can get more flies with honey than with vinegar." Armani watched Carol as she left his office. He noted that her bottom jiggled as she walked across the room and mused to himself, "I bet Carol probably had a little something happening back in her day."

Armani saved the work on his computer and glanced at the clock on the wall. He noticed that it was 7:50 p.m. and realized that the other bosses were probably long gone by now. The firm's hours were 9:00 – 5:00. However, Armani had learned that appearances of long hours were a part of corporate life in America. So to make sure that the powers that be knew he was eager to work, he arrived at 6:00 a.m. sharp every morning and then stayed late every evening. By doing so, he shouted the message, "I am in this thing to win…just like I did when I played football!" Armani's motto was, "Arrive early and leave late, this will determine your pay rate." He learned this lesson quite well when he was a freshman trying to make the team in college. The seniors had this motto plastered on the walls in the gym and they lived by it. Because the senior football players worked hard, laying the groundwork to "get paid" later by the NFL, they set the tone for the work ethic adopted by sophomore and freshman players, and especially Armani.

Armani got up from his desk and grabbed his sport coat, a tailored, navy blue, double-breasted jacket with gold buttons, which perfectly fit his 6 feet, 5-inch frame. Armani was strikingly handsome, physically fit, and weighed 255 pounds. His physique was the result of his coming from a good gene pool. The men in his family all had athletic physiques, like the kind Mohammad Ali had during his peak boxing days. In fact, Armani's father had also been a professional boxer in his younger days. However, his career was cut short when he became unable to win the fight against his own personal demons: alcohol, women, and cocaine.

Armani was not as chiseled as he had been during his playing days, when he weighed 215 pounds. But the extra weight did not look bad on him, especially since he still had a 36-inch waistline. Armani felt that he looked like Denzel this evening, sporting brown, silk slacks, and a cream, silk mock turtleneck sweater with the blue sport coat. The sweater accented his mocha colored skin and his Madison Avenue smile completed the outfit. Looking in the mirror, he thought, "Boy, you're still smooth."

Smooth was the college nickname that he had been tagged with because of the way he ran through open defenders on the football field. Armani caught himself smiling and nodding with approval. Then he heard those voices in his head chastising him. (Still Small Voice: "You know you're full of pride and being boastful." Loud Voice: "Dude, if you got it...you got it. You look good man. Dude you look GOOD!")

Armani had asked Martina to meet him at the bar in the Ritz-Carlton. He liked bringing his dates to the Ritz because the food was excellent and the crowds were not filled with people from his circle of influence. However, most importantly, he would be near nice accommodations just in case he ever wanted to have a more private conversation with them.

Martina was sitting at the bar wearing a black one-piece, tight dress just as Armani had requested. She was a curvaceous, sexy Latina. She had long, cascading black hair and striking features that made her look mature for her age. She was only twenty years old but could look surprisingly sophisticated when she wore her hair up.

Armani had met Martina at the restaurant where she worked in Atlanta. When they met, she thought that she had died and gone to heaven. Though she never admitted this to him, she thought he was simply a bronzed cutie. She knew he was married, but she was not the least bit deterred by that fact. In fact, she thought to herself, "Oh well, he's the one who's married, not me."

As a rule, Martina did not date married men, but she felt that Armani was no ordinary guy. To Martina, he had the popularity of a folk hero whom people loved simply because of his football victories. Martina was fascinated by the attention that Armani got from his fans and she loved the perks and the attention that came her way when she was with him. She felt as if she was out with mafia bad boy. Once, she and Armani had gone to a very exclusive restaurant and their bill was, at least, $200. When Armani tried to pay the tab, the waitress told him that the bill had already been paid by an anonymous benefactor.

Armani approached Martina at the bar. He came up behind her and slid his fingers gently down the nape of her neck, softly whispering in her ear. Speaking slowly and in a deep voice, he said, "Hey, gorgeous. Can I buy you a drink?' Martina turned around and greeted him warmly by pressing her neck against his cheek. Giving him a stern look, she said, "You're too late, buster. Time waits for no man." Armani laughed and said, "I am late and I do apologize." Then he slid onto the bar stool next to her and grabbed her hand. He looked into her eyes and said, "I was…." Martina laughing and shaking her head, she finished the sentence "…tied up at the office?" Armani replied, "See, that's why I like you. You are so smart!"

Armani smiled as he leaned towards the bartender and said, "Jack and Coke, please." The bartender nodded and completed Armani's order. Armani looked around to see if anyone had recognized him. Then he smiled at Martina and asked, "Hey cutie. How was your day?" Martina looked as if she appreciated the offer to share and began, in complete detail, to tell him about the events of her day at work.

Being distracted, all Armani heard was "small tips," "Anna Marie was late," and "Mr. Swanson." What distracted him were his thoughts: (Loud Voice: "Girl, I can't wait to eat so I can get you out of that dress!" Still Small Voice: "Silence.") "Martina continued to talk as Armani continued to nod, smile, and appear to be paying attention.

At one point, Armani drifted back to what Martina was saying, "…so Anna Marie, who is always late…and I'm tired of covering for her." Martina was originally from New York and Armani found her northeastern Spanish accent sexy. He nodded and sipped his drink, knowing that all he had to do was "drop a nickel" in this "juke box" and it would continue to play for hours. Eventually, Armani stopped hearing Martina's voice and tuned into the voices conversing in his own head. (Still Small Voice: "You're in lust." Loud Voice: "Stop thinking…Lust on, big boy. Lust on!")

During the entire time that she had been speaking,

Martina thought she had Armani's undivided attention. She was in heaven and thought to herself, "I could actually fall in love with this guy. I'm constantly thinking about him throughout the day. I wait for him to call with schoolgirl anticipation. He listens to me... Hmmm…could he be the one? I could see us with a house and a three-car garage… being happy together. I know that I could make him forget all that misery that he has with that dreadful wife...They can't have too much invested in each other yet. They've only been married for seven years."

The maître d' came to the bar and informed Armani that their table was ready. Armani told Martina to go ahead and be seated while he took care of the bar tab. She agreed and began to walk briskly to catch up to the young maître d'. Some people sitting near the bar had been watching Armani and Martina. They seemed fascinated by the beautiful Latina lady and continued to watch her as she walked to their table.

Martina seemed to be aware of the attention that she was garnering and she did not disappoint the onlookers. Her walk exuded confidence. After looking back to see if Armani was watching and noticing that he was, she knew she had him mesmerized, so she walked with even more emphasis. Armani noted Martina's actions and then looked at the bartender, who was watching her as well. Armani smiled at him while paying him, just to let him know that it was okay for him to check out his date and that he was not bothered by it.

Armani did not mind the attention that Martina drew. After all, one of the reasons that he was attracted to her was that she was gorgeous. Armani got a charge when other men looked admiringly at her—as long as they followed the rule of "You can lust, but you had better not touch!"

Unexpectedly, Armani's mind drifted to Shelia and he recalled how she used to grab a crowd's attention—back before she had their daughter, Sierra. Shelia had long legs and a basketball player's frame. Yep. His wife was quite the stunner in her day too. But since she had the baby, her shape was not quite as appealing to him as it had been, and he really did not feel about her the way that he used to…At least, this was the main reason that he used to justify why he "needed" to cheat. The runner-up excuse was that the chemistry that he once had with his wife was gone.

The bottom line for Armani was that he was unsatisfied in his marriage, his feeling was a moving truck had backed up to his house and dispatched movers to snatch the happiness right out of his and Shelia's relationship. He chuckled and thought they hauled, "A*S with the romance too." Remembering the feeling that he got when he saw how his wife's presence commanded attention and now seeing people check out his lovely Martina, Armani stuck out his chest just a little further, like old times.

Armani snapped back to reality and gazed around, searching for the shortest route to the table where Martina was seated. Some of the men gazed in his direction, and then quickly looked down and away. Some of the women also looked at him, but quickly averted their eyes when he looked back at them.

Having spent quite a good bit of time on the social

scene, Armani had noticed that "sistas" are quick to look at black men. But when the men return the look, the women quickly look away, like they'd been caught stealing. However, the bold sisters will look a man straight in his eyes, especially when they seem to be bothered by the fact that a black brother is dating outside of his race.

Gazing at those women who were staring at him and giving him a hateful look, Armani return looked to stated, "Trick, I could buy you!" Once Armani realized that he did not recognize anyone and that no one seemed to recognize him, he held his head high and vainly strutted off. While walking away, Armani could hear those voices in his head speaking. (Still Small Voice: "I hate a vain look!" Loud Voice: "Stop thinking…start smiling!")

When Armani found Martina, she was seated and was gesturing to him to sit next to her. Armani took the chair, but pulled it out so that his long legs would fit under the table. He then surveilled the room once again to ensure that he did not see any co-workers, friends, or anyone else that might tell Shelia about his little secret.

Not seeing anyone who seemed familiar to him, Armani placed his napkin on his lap, adjusted his chair, and looked back around the room again. Then he thought to himself, "Good. No one here I know. There's a cute couple, but that dude is worried about his girl checking me. Those two old ladies are just chatting, so it's all green lights. Ok, now I can be myself, especially now that the Jack Daniel's has taken effect."

Turning his focus back to Martina, Armani said, "It's really crowded in here. The Atlanta night scene is growing." Martina looked around, nodding in agreement. Then Armani leaned towards Martina and smelled her hair. He smiled and shrugged his shoulders and said, "Girl, you smell delightful!" Martina blushed and smiled. She was pleased, knowing that Armani obviously appreciated good fragrances because he always smelled so great. Martina had really wanted to choose a scent that would make him think of her when he recalled this evening.

Still smiling and looking at Armani, Martina asked, "So what do you feel like having for dinner, Mani?" Armani grabbed the menu, starred at it with a puzzled look on his face, and then said, "I'm not sure. Probably some fish. I don't want anything heavy." Smiling and gazing lustfully at Martina's lap and chest, Armani thought, "I don't want to tire too soon..."

Just as he was about to explore his train of thought further, once again he heard from those voices in his head. (Still Small Voice: "You are lusting after this woman!" Loud Voice: "Remember, foot massages really turn her on!") Seeing the look on Armani's face, Martina smiled and coyly said, "Armani...you devil." Armani grinned and tried to ignore the nagging voices in his head vying for his attention. (Still Small Voice: "You know you are in lust and you're sinning!" Loud Voice: "Yeah, maybe. But it feels good and I intend to be into more than sin by the end of the night.")

CHAPTER 2

HELEN AND DEXTER

Helen Lewis was a beautiful, light-skinned black woman. She had a head full of thick black hair, the same as her mother and maternal grandmother had. She was very confident, secure in her career, and not easily intimidated.

It was a Monday morning and Helen had a ton of things that she needed to get done for this day. She was trying to get into the office early but her day had gotten off to a slow start. Her hair was still a mess and she had not even begun to apply her makeup.

Realizing by this point that she was going to be late, she began to go over in her mind her appointments for the day. She remembered that she needed to see the school principal at Wilkerson Elementary School. She had stopped by his office on Friday to get him to sign an attendance form that she needed to take to the meeting with her supervisor that afternoon. Helen had missed the principal on Friday and wondered if he had signed the form, which she needed in order to close out the Washington case today.

The Washington dependency case was one of the biggest cases that Helen had been assigned as a supervisor with the Harris County Department of Human Services. The judge in the case wanted to terminate parental rights, but Helen felt that it would be best for the children if the mother was given another chance. Maybe she would come to her senses and to put her life on the right track. Jessie, the mother, had two beautiful children who unfortunately were not her top priorities. Helen felt that though Jessie professed to love her children, her actions indicated that she preferred to chase after her irresponsible boyfriend. She was truly stuck on stupid.

Distracted by her thoughts, Helen peered through her blinds and looked outside. As she felt herself becoming irritated, she heard the voices in her head speaking about the condition of the yard. (Loud Voice: "Look at that grass, all over the place, and the crab grass too." Still Small Voice: "It just needs trimming.") Realizing what she had been thinking, she became furious within herself and she began to frown.

Helen shook her head to try to clear out the voices. However, they would not be quieted and they continued to speak. (Loud Voice: "Look at the Smith's grass across the street. See how neat and clean their yard is?" Still Small Voice: "It's just grass.") "What a sorry husband I have!" she thought! Then she said out loud, "Look at the Smith's grass across the street. Just look at how neat and clean their yard is."

As Helen was deciding what to do with her hair, she reminded herself to make an appointment with her stylist, Shania. Brushing her hair and finding resistance, she realized that she needed a touch up, soon. Helen looked in the mirror at her hair and pondered her hairstyle. She then thought about the younger black women and their resorting to the use of hair weaves.

Helen looked approvingly at her hair length and smiled to herself, thinking, "It's still a pretty good length."

She decided long ago that she would never succumb to the pressure to have long hair just because she could buy it. Helen had also decided that, for her, it was far more important that she had her hair, rather than horse hair.

Helen did not really have an appreciation for the fascination that some black women seemed to have with having long hair. She had only dated black men and felt that they really appreciated women who wore their hair own hair in appealing styles. At least that was what several men had told her. From what Helen had learned, it seemed that whether a woman's length hair was short, medium, or long, black men just wanted you to keep it real and keep it done!

Helen, who should have been getting ready for work, once again found herself distracted and looking through the blinds at her yard. She was thinking, "Why can't he just hire someone to cut the grass? If he did, I wouldn't be so upset all the time about the yard. He's not working as much this summer, so he's got more time to spend on keeping it up. Men… they all want nice things, but they don't want to put forth the effort to maintain them!"

Helen found herself wondering why men could not understand that just like a woman's hair is a reflection of her personality; her home is also an expression of herself. Frowning, Helen shifted her weight from one foot to the other as the voices in her head began shouting to gain her attention. (Loud Voice: "And if it wasn't for you, he wouldn't have any grass!" Still Small Voice: "It's just grass.") Then she said aloud, "If it had not been for my credit, we wouldn't even have a house, let alone any grass!"

Now Helen found herself in a state of gloomy discontentment concerning her marriage. She did not feel that Dexter was as affectionate with her or as invested in their marriage as he had once been. Sensing that their marriage was in trouble, Helen asked Dexter to go to marriage counseling with her and he agreed.

The marriage counselor said that she and Dexter had encountered a "wall" in their marriage and told them that they could either tear down the wall or the wall was going to tear them down. The therapist also reminded them that marriages face all types of challenges, some of which would involve petty issues and others of which would involve more serious ones.

In an effort to help Helen find balance and significance in her life and marriage, the counselor urged Helen not to allow the petty things to upset her as easily as they had in the past. (Loud Voice in Helen's Head: "She probably got a real man at home!" Still Small Voice: "It's just grass.") Reflecting on the counselor's advice, Helen said, "Hmmph…she's probably has a gardener. What does she know?!"

After a few sessions, Helen could see that the meetings were a waste of time because; Dexter was no longer making an effort to incorporate any of the changes suggested in their discussions. Thinking about the last session and becoming upset, Helen thought, "All he does is sit there like a bump on a log and listen to me restate how stupid he is. What the counselor and I say seems to go in one ear and right out of the other."

Frowning and becoming very angry, she thought, "Dexter's biggest problem is that he's a momma's boy and always will be. He doesn't know how to fix anything around this house and has no clue as to how to maintain or keep up a car." Then she thought, "All the other men I knew were handy around the house."

Helen believed that Dexter's problem was related to a lack of guidance and no home training. Then she thought, "His real problem is that he never received anything from that boxer-want-to-be-crack head daddy of his. If a real man walked into this house, Dexter wouldn't know it, even if the man slapped him! My mother told me not to marry his sorry A*S. She knew he was a mamma's boy when she met him. She told me that she could tell because he was too docile for her likings. She also pointed out that a real man wouldn't let me talk to him the way that I spoke to Dexter." Helen was kind of shaken as she reflected over the conversation that she and her mother had about her marrying Dexter. At the time that she and Dexter were dating, she felt that Dexter was "allowing" her to have input about the things that were important to her, but her mother told her that she was running him. When Dexter proposed to her, Helen thought marrying him was the right thing to do. More than that, she was ready to get married because a lot of her friends were doing it.

Like any other woman, Helen wanted the man that she married to be a good provider and, when Dexter proposed, accepting seemed to be a good idea because she thought that he and his family were well off. She based her assumption on the beautiful home that he lived in and on the nice car that he drove. What Helen found out after they were married was that it was Dexter's brother, Armani, who was well off as the result of his NFL signing bonus and that Dexter was driving Armani's car.

After she and Dexter were married, Helen found out that Dexter was not wealthy at all, but it was too late to do anything except try to make the best of the situation. Helen had decided that being married to Dexter could not be all that bad, especially considering that they got along pretty well. Dexter earned a fairly decent salary working as an elementary school basketball coach. She figured that eventually, with a little prodding from her, Dexter would advance his career to the college ranks where we would make some real money.

Helen's thoughts were disrupted by the buzzing of her cell phone. She looked at the caller ID and decided to let the call go to voicemail. On the screen were the initials DHS, but Helen knew that it was not really an office call. She had placed the number of the caller under the name Department of Human Services (DHS) for secrecy. Just in case Dexter happened to see the caller ID, he would think the call was just routine. Staring at her cell phone, Helen took a deep breath and shook her head. She knew that the call was from Mr. Brandon Wilkes.

Helen had just recently met this man at her office when he had stopped her to ask directions to an office in her building. Helen was preoccupied when Mr. Wilkes stopped her and asked for help, but she most definitely noticed him and thought, "He is fine without trying!" as the women in the office would say.

After Helen directed him to his destination, Mr. Wilkes thanked her for assisting him and seemed to be more interested in taking her to lunch than in finding the office that he had just asked about. Though Helen was intrigued by the idea of socializing with him, she declined his lunch invitation. She thought it would not look right for her, a married woman, to accept a stranger's lunch offer without good reason. Also, being the frequent object of men's attention, Helen was used to being hit on by men and was, therefore, not particularly moved by Mr. Wilkes' interest in taking her to lunch.

In response to his lunch invitation, Helen explained to Mr. Wilkes that she did not accept lunch dates with virtual strangers. Though he understood her reason for saying no, Mr. Wilkes was not ready to quit just yet, and was determined to try again. Later during the week, he called Helen, having located her office number by her ID badge. Their conversation was short and cordial. Mr. Wilkes again asked Helen for a lunch date and, once again, she declined.

Mr. Wilkes was not deterred by Helen's rejection of his offer to take her to lunch. In fact, he was more intrigued than ever and continued to call her. During their brief conversations, Helen and Mr. Wilkes talked about his work, his expectations of being promoted, and the spotty dating scenes of his life. His calls were becoming the bright spots of Helen's days and, eventually, she actually began looking forward to the cat-and-mouse interaction between him and herself, especially on those days when Dexter really "worked" her nerves.

Eventually, she and Mr. Wilkes did go to lunch together. But afterwards, Helen would not allow him to escort her to back to her building. Though her plan was to avoid getting too friendly with Mr. Wilkes, on one occasion—when Dexter had gone out of town on a recruiting trip—Helen did give Mr. Wilkes her cell phone number.

Helen's logic for sharing her number and for allowing Mr. Wilkes to stick his foot a little further in her door was that, in Dexter's absence, she felt rather lonely and wanted someone to talk with. All things considered, Mr. Wilkes would not be a bad choice to make her feel better. So that she could continue to control the situation, when she gave Mr. Wilkes her cell phone number, and not her home number, she made it clear to him that although she wanted to hear from him, he could not just call her anytime and that she would let him know when he could call.

However lately she began having more and more conversations with her new friend on her cell phone. In her mind, she justified her behavior based on the tension at home; the marriage counseling was not helping her problems with Dexter; AND, most importantly, Mr. Wilkes actually made her smile. When she got up this morning, she thought that maybe today if she finished up early, she might allow him to take her to lunch. Well, so much for that plan. Having to meet with her supervisor today after lunch, she allowed Brandon's call to go to her voicemail.

Peering out of her side windows and seeing a lawn service truck, Helen thought, "The grass is greener on the other side of the fence because the neighbors have BEST-LAWN to come out and periodically treat their grass!" Because she and Dexter were on a tight budget, they could not afford a commercial lawn care service. "Now, look!" she thought. "The crab grass is all over the walkway, in the back of the house. I think it's time for Mr. Lewis to get a call!"

*****

Just across town, Dexter Lewis looked around his office at Lamar High School and noticed that the dust was starting to pile up around his Miracle Mile trophy. He was in his third year at Lamar and relished his freshmen coaching successes as if they had just occurred yesterday.

As the freshman basketball coach at Lamar, Dexter was very proud of the team's accomplishments. He had taken a no-name team, initially placed at the bottom of its conference, to the state finals championship tournament. Although they lost the championship game by three points due to a blown call by the officiating crew, the journey to the finals was well worth the trip.

Though they missed grabbing the "gold," the mostly freshman team took second place. The silver-place trophy was a symbol of the team being audacious enough to hope. The team had played in the championship tournament and had dared to believe that they could win. Dexter wanted to keep the trophy in his office, instead of in the school trophy case, as a symbol of faith and the evidence of what tenacious pursuit could yield.

Dexter's concentration was broken by the sound of the phone ringing. He answered with, "Coach Lewis."

School was out for the summer break and Dexter came to the office just to get away from the house whenever he thought his wife was working there. Coming from the receiver, Dexter heard a loud, excited voice say, "DEXTER MAURICE LEWIS!" "Yes, Helen. I'm at the office," Dexter responded dryly. Helen continued sternly, "I'm not checking on you, mister. I just wanted to remind you that the grass needs cutting." The next thing he heard was a loud click, following by a dial tone. Dexter looked at the receiver, looked at the wall, then looked up and shook his head, thinking, "I know that the counseling sessions stressed the importance of getting to the point in their discussions, but Helen was taking this a little too far."

Dexter and Helen had been married for four years and they had no children. Early in their marriage, they did not have too many disagreements. They experienced the usual petty marital differences. Over time, however, those small differences had evolved into more challenging problems, especially after they learned that Helen had a tilted uterus that prevented her from conceiving. The infertility issue resulted in additional stress on their marriage because there was a procedure that have could cured the condition. However, it involved an expensive operation that they could not afford.

After Helen hung up on him, Dexter thought, "Helen is always on me about spending more time with her, but when I do, all we end up doing is arguing. She nags me about every little thing and, it seems that she's never happy anymore."

Dexter loved Helen and felt that, if he could fix

their problems, he would. But whatever was troubling Helen was something that was beyond his understanding. Though he was not a Christian per se, he thought that whatever the problem with Helen was, it must have been spiritual.

Dexter's thought that there was a God, somewhere, but that God did not play a part in his day-to-day life. Reflecting on the question of the existence of God, Dexter thought, "Who knows?" Smiling, he said to himself, "God, if you are real, could you help us?" An uncomfortable chill came over Dexter and he seemed to hear voices in his head speaking to him. (Still Small Voice: "Dexter, I am very real." Loud Voice: "That's BULLSH*T! Blah, Blah, Blah, Blah...!")

After Helen's call, Dexter decided to take some balls out and do a shoot around to get the ol' blood pumping. The sound of the bouncing balls was like music to his ears. Dexter was an all star athlete in his day. In his youth, with his lanky slim frame, a lot of people thought that he maybe would play professional basketball one day.

As Dexter advanced through school, he quickly found out that in organized sports, the defense could easily expose a player's weaknesses. In his case, it had become obvious that he could not effectively handle the ball with his left hand. When he played, the defenders would play him to his right and force him to go left. When forced to go left, his hand-to-eye coordination would be limited. Being right hand-oriented, he could not dribble, pass the ball efficiently, or shoot with his left hand.

Because of Dexter's left hand liability, the high

school coaches began limiting his playing time and basically used him for pick-up minutes when a game was well out of reach. Knowing that an effective basketball player had to be ambidextrous, Dexter realized that he would not likely make it to the pros, understanding all too well that a point guard who could not go left was a liability to any team.

Bounce, bounce, bounce. Dexter shot....Swish. All net with no rim. Bounce... Bounce. While dribbling the ball on the court and running towards the goal, Dexter was thinking, "It isn't as if I don't want to cut the grass. But she makes me feel like I'm going to get a whipping if I don't cut the grass...like she's my momma..." Dexter was trying to concentrate on shooting the ball, but he was distracted by the voices speaking in his head. (Still Small Voice: "Dexter, what's wrong with just cutting the grass if it needs to be done?" Loud Voice: "Look, you are no momma's boy...and what's wrong with her hands anyway?")

Bounce, bounce, bounce. Dexter shot....The ball hit the backboard and bounced off the rim... Bounce... Bounce. Dexter was trying to remember the last time that he and Helen made love...or even had sex. It had been so long that he could not even remember the occasion. The romance was gone from their marriage and the counseling had not resurrected any positive emotions so far. Dexter really could not grasp the purpose of the counseling sessions so he did not participate fully in them. He justified his attitude, thinking, "Marriage counseling is for women."

Frustrated at the tension and disconnect between Helen and himself, Dexter found himself lamenting,

"Women seem to remember every detail and every moment of every incident, as if they have an internal calendar for recording the negative." Mystified and vexed, Dexter wondered why all that he could seem to recall in counseling sessions was the fact that at home, he was getting no sex, no cooking was going on, and there was no peace. Helen, however, could give the counselor specifics concerning dates and times things happened. She could even remember the responses that we both had in those situations, and even what I was wearing.

From her comments in counseling, it seemed that Helen's biggest complaints had to do with housecleaning, house maintenance, and money. Since Helen never cleaned or did any major work around the house, Dexter was not sure why she felt compelled to complain about the house being dirty. And as to money, even though Helen was the primary bread winner, she had not always been. Before she received the promotion at DHS, they had earned about the same salary. However, when Helen was promoted to supervisor, she earned a lot more than Dexter, even after adding in the significant raise that Dexter received when he was promoted to a high school coach.

One reason that Dexter could not grasp Helen's complaints about making more money was because Dexter did not believe that a man had to make more money than the woman. As for himself, he was happy all the way to bank regardless of who in the household earned the most money. His feeling was, "As long as the lights were on and the bills were paid, it was all good!"

Bounce, bounce, bounce, Dexter shot...The ball hit

the front of the rim and bounced back to him...bounce, bounce. Dexter felt that Helen was looking at her girl-friends' lives and was comparing her life to theirs. Her friends were successful business women who had professional jobs. Some had married pretty successful businessmen who had their own companies.

Dexter could not usually relate to Helen's complaints about status because he did not measure success the way that Helen and her friends seemed to. To them, success was measured by their clothes, their cars, and their houses. To Dexter, success was seeing his players' eyes light up when they finally caught on to a play on the court or when they got the idea in their head that, "to win, you must trust your team mates."

Dexter had at first thought their goals in marriage were equal. Though Helen desired money and social position, when she graduated from college, rather than to pursue a financially lucrative career, she chose to follow her heart's dream and become a social worker. Dexter applauded Helen for following her dreams to assist people.

A few years after getting married, they were finally able to afford to get the house that she wanted, albeit it was a starter home. Though Helen was already looking forward to the next house, Dexter felt proud of their home and was in no hurry to rush to purchase another one, thinking that even though the house may not have been their ultimate house, at least they were not living in an apartment anymore.

As Dexter reflected over the move into their current house, he thought over the fact that he and Helen had not moved because he objected to apartment living. Dexter was thinking, "In fact, living in an apartment was not so bad. We seemed happier and closer then. We shared one car and we had to 'penny-up' to get pizza. But we were happy in those days together. We were certainly a lot happier than we are now. Here we are living in a nice house, driving two cars, but it seems that all we got with more stuff, has been more stuff problems."

Shooting the ball and smiling, Dexter thought, "When we were in the apartment, the bills got paid, didn't they? Then he thought, "I may not be as driven as she is about keeping my credit intact, but, hey, you can't take your credit rating to your grave."

Bounce, bounce, bounce, Dexter shot...swish. All net, no rim. Bounce...bounce. While standing at the free throw line, Dexter was thinking to himself, "Still got my stroke... I'm still the Cane." Cane was the nickname given to Dexter back in his elementary school days in New Orleans. It was short for Hurricane and was a reference to Dexter's ability to blow by his defenders like a hurricane. The name was shortened to Cane when one of the Booster Club members prepared a sign that read "Cane is Able."

Absentmindedly, Dexter found himself just dribbling and not taking any shots. He kept being distracted by disjointed thoughts running and up down the courts of his mind. As he tried to shoot the ball a final time, Dexter began to focus in on the voices that he heard speaking in his head. (Still Small Voice: "Dexter, don't forget the grass." Loud Voice: "C'mon kid. Keep stroking that rock. You're on a roll, Cane!")

From his perspective, Dexter had really tried to make Helen happy. When things began deteriorating in their relationship, he figured that, if he had made more money, Helen would be happier. So when an opening came up at Lamar, he lobbied hard for the position. He knew that his credentials were lacking because he did not have a college degree. Feeling a bit insecure because of that, when he applied for the job, he thought that his chances of actually landing it were just as slim as he was.

Dexter was also dubious of his chances of being hired because he knew that coaches were usually hired from within their own circle of coaching friends. He also realized that, had it not been for his brother's connections with the mayor of Houston, he would never have been granted an interview, nor would he have gotten the coaching job. The new position allowed him and Helen to save for the down payment on the house in which they were presently living.

"We had good times, back then, in the apartment and we had no grass to cut." Dexter thought. Dexter recalled that when he came home, Helen would have food on the table, candles would be lit, and music would be playing. He and Helen would sit for hours and talk about floor plans, designs for the bedroom furniture, and plans for their future. "We had plans and goals and we were happy." *Bounce, bounce, bounce. Dexter shot the ball and hit the back board.* The ball bounced off the rim…bounce…bounce). "Now, we argue over what channel to watch on TV, who's going to cook, AND THAT D*M GRASS!"

Dexter tried to figure out when the problems

started. He really could not put his finger on when, where, or how they began. He knew that they had started slowly and that they had built up over time. At one point, Dexter and Helen had tried going to church in an effort to improve their marriage. Dexter, believing that going to church would heal all their wounds, suggested that they make a regular practice of attending Sunday services together and even attending couples Bible study. He was looking for a miracle from God in his marriage.

The only revelation that Dexter had received from going to church with Helen was that on the way to church, they seemed to argue more. Believing that continuing to go would only lead to more arguing and would only put an additional strain on their marriage, Shelia said, "No thanks!" to his suggestion of more intense church participation as a couple.

Though Dexter was not sure just what had gone wrong in his and Helen's marriage, he was sure of one thing: The fun was just got up and left their relationship. Dexter just did not like being around Helen anymore. She made him feel small especially when she called him Lil Man and that really hurt. He thought that wives were supposed to build up their men, not tear them down.

Though he understood that marriage would have moments filled with all types of emotions and challenges, Dexter still believed that marriage was supposed to be fun sometimes … at least, on the weekends. Perplexed and having no more clarity on the deteriorated state of his marriage than he had before he began shooting hoops, Dexter thought, shaking his head in frustration, "Maybe women are only happy when they're shopping." Dexter paused and looked at his watch. "It's 9:00. In eight hours it will be time to go home and face the silence."

CHAPTER 3

CHALLENGES

Shelia Lewis was quite the professional. Having majored in business, she graduated magna cum laude from the University of Georgia Tech. Since graduation, she had excelled at the jobs she'd had, and she was currently working in the banking industry. Staring out of her corner office window, Shelia reflected over the past and thought to herself, "I have died on gone to Heaven. I never dreamed that I would be head of the operations department at a major bank by the age of thirty."

As she pondered her success, Shelia was amazed by the gossip and rumors floating around the office. They were saying that the only reason that she had climbed the corporate ladder so quickly was because she was married to Armani Lewis, also known as Mr. Smooth from Georgia Tech. She was proud of being married to Armani, but she knew—and wanted it to be clearly understood—that her success in the corporate world was the result of old fashioned hard work and grit. Usually Shelia did not even allow herself to be bothered by such gossip, but she had to admit that she was annoyed by this particular rumor because it was not true. She thought out loud, "If those haters only knew how many long hours I spent studying, or the many countless hours I stayed up trying to find the two pennies that were needed to reconcile a problem for my macro accounting homework!"

While in school, Shelia not only worked hard to be the best that she could be, she also worked hard to help others in the areas that she had mastered. What she realized was that when she helped others to learn, she herself learned the most. "Hmmmph," she thought, still staring out of the window, "I did not receive an honor graduate ring because of Smooth! I worked hard for my accomplishments! I wish they understood that! As for Mr. Lewis, I never pursued him. He pursued me…and he did not do too badly in getting me!" She then smiled.

Armani Lewis was Mister Everything at Tech and was a sure first round draft choice for the NFL. But before Shelia and Armani had formally met, the women had been all over him. Shelia noticed him back then, but she never thought to approach him because she felt that his head was too big to fit in the same room with himself, let alone with her. But even though Shelia paid him no attention to him, somehow, Armani found her.

Shelia was definitely a stunning beauty. She was 5 feet10 inches tall, blonde, and very attractive. While Shelia knew that Armani had noticed her long legs, cascading blonde hair, and overall good looks, she knew that those were not the characteristics that drew him to her. Instead, Armani had fallen in love with her spirit. With his college fame, good looks, and potential to earn lots of money, he could have had any woman on campus that he desired. He was attracted to her because she was humble of heart, and he thought he could trust her.

When Armani began pursuing Shelia, he thought that he was "the stuff" and Shelia perceived that if he thought that, then he truly wasn't. After the first time that he approached her, Shelia decided that she definitely had no interest in becoming a part of his harem. Although he continued to try to engage her, Shelia politely declined his advances. Though Shelia picked up on Armani's high opinion of himself, she had no idea that he was the good in football as he was. She certainly didn't know that he was a first round draft choice and soon to be millionaire until her girlfriend, Amy, told her.

Although Shelia's initial reason for rebuffing Armani's advances was his attitude, there was another reason—the fact that he was black. Shelia was not a bigot and she had never been taught to dislike or avoid black people. However, in her community, dating black men was not encouraged either.

Even after seven years of marriage, there were still moments when Shelia was uncomfortable being in public with Armani. Not because she was ashamed of being with him, but because there were often the disapproving looks that she got from black women when they were together. "UGH!" she thought. Those sisters would often give her the coldest and harshest looks! They acted as if she had stolen their golden goose right from under their noses!

Shelia smiled as she thought about the fact that Armani loved the attention that they would get whenever they went anywhere together. He would deliberately hold her hands and kiss her right in front of the sisters just to infuriate them. There were others besides some black women who seemed less than thrilled to see Armani and Shelia together. Many white guys responded negatively to their relationship. They often would give Shelia disapproving looks as if to say, "There goes another dumb blonde stuck on another black football player's jock." Shelia felt certain that they probably never considered that she was a woman of substance and intelligence. They didn't realize that she was with Armani because she loved him, not because she was a mindless "Barbie" who just flocked behind him because he was on his way up.

Once Armani convinced her that he was serious about a future together, Shelia no longer saw him as just another vain football player; she saw him as man with vision. Once she saw that, she no longer really cared about what people thought about black or white. Before getting married, they dated for three years. During that time, she was walking on clouds. Armani was very courteous. He walked her to class, held her books, and called her all the time. He was a gentleman and she never wanted for anything. He would bring her ice cream at night and would take her out to eat on Friday nights if he did not have late practices or a game on Saturday. There were a lot of envious women on campus and rumors were rampant that Shelia and Armani were sleeping together, but that was not the case. Shelia told Armani that she wanted to wait a while and he honored that. He put her on a pedestal.

As Shelia began to zone back to reality, she found herself frowning and thinking aloud, "...and that is exactly where he left me...on a pedestal, at home alone, with a three-year-old child!" Shelia, of course, loved her daughter, Sierra. But that young lady was certainly a handful! Armani pretty much left Sierra's care to Shelia and, quite frankly, she resented it. No one but God knew the hell that Armani had been putting Sierra and her through. Besides not helping as he ought to with household chores, he constantly argued with her and was jealous whenever other men looked at her, especially white men.

Yes, Mr. Armani Lewis had been a fine gentleman in college, when he thought that he was going pro and thought that he stood to make a huge amount of money in the NFL. But things quickly changed when his dreams of playing in the NFL were shattered, after he tore his anterior cruciate ligament (ACL) in his knee of his senior year. The injury required immediate surgery. Although the procedure and subsequent rehabilitation had gone well, Armani was never able to execute his explosive moves as he had done prior to the injury.

After Armani realized the impact of the damage to his knee, he changed. He had been paid a two million dollar signing bonus, but for two years he could not make the first squad of the team that drafted him. Subsequently, he could not even make any NFL practice squad. All of these events contributed to Armani losing his self-confidence, feeling like a failure, and becoming a very bitter man. Even after he began to treat her differently, Shelia never gave up on him because it was not the lure of money or a grand lifestyle that she fell in love with. It was the man himself. She prayed for God to help them adjust to the change in their circumstances.

Shelia had not known very many black men before meeting Armani. However, among the ones that she had met or had watched on TV, she detected that Armani had a certain something. It was a manly swagger. Shelia was drawn to Armani by that certain type of old school confidence he possessed. She could not put her finger on what "it" was, but the closest word she could find to describe "it" was "charisma!"

When they began dating, Shelia and Armani spent so much time together that people thought they were joined at the hip. Although she felt many people stereotyped and reduced their relationship to, "blonde white woman gets with black man for money or great sex." She wondered if anyone ever considered that she could fall in love with a man because he was kind and loving and they shared the same dreams.

Shelia was jolted back to reality by the buzzing sound from her cell phone, which was on vibrate mode. Shelia recognized the caller ID then answered the telephone and said, "Hey, girl. How are you? Yes, I will be there at 6:00 p.m. No, it's in Buckhead, adjacent to the Cheesecake Factory... Yes, on ...yes...right there on the corner... Okay...I will see you then." Shelia and her girlfriend Tonya had planned a girl's night out. Shelia decided that she needed a break from work and home. She needed a break from being "every woman" at home and from the cooking and cleaning, from being a care taker, and yes, from the arguing. She needed a drink with a good old friend and Tonya was just the person to get away with.

Shelia had met Tonya four years ago while in training at Citizen's Bank. Tonya was no longer at the bank because she had been fired over a credit card fraud incident, which Tonya swore she had nothing to do with. Tonya's profession of innocence did not save her though. Shelia believed that, ultimately, she was fired because the incident had tainted her credentials. In the banking industry, suspicion of guilt is just as bad has actually being guilty, especially—according to Tonya—if you are a black person.

Shelia was glad that she knew Tonya. She was a good friend to have, especially in pretentious Atlanta where lifestyle was far more important than substance of character. After college, Shelia found that it was hard for her to make long-term female friends. The main obstacles seemed to be other women's jealousy not only of Shelia's beauty but also of her drive to achieve her career goals and her dream life style. To Shelia's great delight, she and Tonya were great companions for each other because Tonya was not intimidated by Shelia, nor was she jealous of her ambition. Besides Tonya being attractive herself, she was very level-headed, had a great sense of humor, and was just a fun person to hang out and relax.

She had gotten very close with Tonya's when they started attending the same church in College Park. Tonya had gone with her a few times and then Shelia started going on her own when she found out that the people in the church did not seem to care that she was white. Not only did they not seem to care, they acted as if they were not in church to see anybody but Jesus. Shelia fell in love with the pastor and his message about the "Still Small Voice" of God, so she joined the church and even became active in the children's ministry.

Shelia looked at her cell phone for the correct time. She saw that it was 5:30 p.m. She picked up the phone and dialed Armani's cell phone number. Speaking joyfully, she said, "Heeeey! Pookie Pookie!" … Armani answered his cell phone, using a business tone. "Hey, Shelia. Wassup? I'm kind of…" Shelia, interrupting him said, "…busy, I know baby…I won't hold you long, but baby I have a meeting with Mr. Coleman and my branch personnel manager after work."

As Shelia stumbled over the words that she had just spoken, she became aware of voices speaking in her head. (Still Small Voice: "Shelia, you know that's a lie. You do not have a meeting." Louder Voice: "It's only a white lie and it is a meeting! With Tonya!") "It shouldn't take any longer than an hour or so. So baby...do you mind picking up Sierra today?" Pleeeassse, Pookie Poo!" Armani was silent for a moment. Then he asked, "So what time will you be home? "Well, the meeting is at 6:00, so I should be there by 7:30 or 8:00 p.m. at the latest…and baby, please feed my baby girl. You know that she gets that ferocious appetite from her big ol' daddy'!" Kiss... kiss…smooches!"

Shelia hung up the phone, not really listening for an answer, because she knew that Armani would pick up his daughter. Shelia thought, "He may take me through hell, but that man loves his little girl with all his heart. And why wouldn't he? Sierra looks just like him!" Sierra had long, flowing, jet black hair and a year-round tan that gave her the look of being of Latin descent. Shelia smiled and thought, "She's quite a cute little girl, if I may say so myself!" Shelia's satisfaction with herself for getting through that white lie to Armani was interrupted by those persistent voices that had become regular visitors in her head. (Still

Small Voice: "Shelia, liars shall not tarry in My eyesight."
Loud Voice: "It's a white lie. It's a white lie."). In response
to the voices, Shelia said aloud, "I know. Lord, please forgive me. Please help me not do it again!"

Shelia's voices were not the only ones that felt like
speaking. Those in Armani's head had also become vocal.
(Loud Voice: "HOW DARE THIS B@%CH, CALL YOU
AT THE LAST MINUTE, WITH THIS BULLS@#T, LIKE
YOU ARE SOME PUNK BOY!" Still Small Voice:
"Sierra's your daughter too!") Armani was so mad he
cursed out loud. He thought, "How dare she call me and
ask me, at the last minute, to go get her daughter!"

Armani flipped open his cell phone and began dial-
ing as he also heard voices in his head. (Still Small Voice:
"Break the date." Loud Voice: "Don't break the date, just
postpone it.") When his call was answered, Armani said,
"Tina, what's up, baby girl? Look, I'm going to have to
push back our meeting to more like 9:00." He paused, listening to the voices in his head. (Still Small Voice: "Tell the
truth!" Loud Voice: "LIE!"). "Yeah, girl," chuckling, "I
have to meet with a few colleagues after work." Tina
replied, "Ok, Mani. I will see you around…what? 9:00
p.m.?" Armani replied, "No. Let's make it 9:30 to be on the
safe side if that's okay with you?" Tina responded, "Okay."
Armani said, "I will see you then." Tina said, seductively,
"Armani…I have a lil surprisssse for you…" Intrigued, Armani asked, "What is it, Miss Tina?" Tina, speaking like a
little kid, replied, "You'll just have to wait, won't you?!"
Armani laughed and replied, "I guess so…Ciao, babe."

After he hung up with Tina, Armani saved the file

he was working on and logged off his computer. The Seligman file had been put to bed. "Another alligator off my desk for now," he thought. Files like the Seligman were called "alligators" because they required a large investment of time, but had not yet yielded a monetary return for the company. Until an advertising campaign made money for the company, it was considered an alligator that could come back to bite you. No one wanted these files because the unwritten rule for junior vice executives was that three alligators in a year and you are out of the swamp!

The bottom line policy at Armani's company was that the goal of business is money. If any employee does not make money for "Mount Rushmore" (the name given to Lawson's elite all-white board of directors), that person would be replaced with someone else who could. Lawson was all about milking as much money out of a campaign as possible. They had to spend money upfront to create the initial advertisement pitch for the customer. The amount of money invested by Lawson on research, development, and production for each campaign was astronomical.

Once a client has decided to purchase its advertising campaign with the firm, the next step was to determine whether the campaign had achieved the desired effect on sales growth or a "spike" in sales from the target audience. In the advertising arena, to win an advertising account is to win the game but to win with a spike is paramount to winning the Super Bowl. The bigger the ad account, the bigger the desired spike and the smaller the desired period of time for achieving the spike.

To Armani this was gridiron football pure and simple, and he loved it. Typically, it was about two weeks after an ad was placed before sponsor analysts would call and report on whether there had been a spike in sales growth. Armani found those two weeks nerve-racking, but so far, his production ads with the firm had been stellar. Some of the executives at the firm were dubious of Armani's advertising skills. Many attributed his good production rate to the fact he had been given existing accounts for large well-established products.

It worked out that a lot of the large accounts owners were football junkies and had followed Armani's career. Generally, it seemed that they believed that if Smooth was on their team, there would be no way they could lose. But Armani tried to keep a level head and not get too pumped up by all the hype because he understood that by many in the industry he was viewed as being a lucky a black man. He understood that even for those ad executives who liked his style on the football field, at the end of his day, the only field that mattered was the spike field.

Armani knew that before clients would invest a dime in his company, the ad products definitely had to be carefully thought out, easily explainable, understandable, and then marketable. With that in mind, he relentlessly poured over account details to better understand how to analyze a market. He also met time and time again with the design team to ensure that the product to be presented to account executives made good business sense. Armani felt that after he had prepared and executed a thorough strategy for winning an account, then he could flash his movie star smile, overpower the client with his charm, and "run the ball into the end zone" for a "touchdown."

Because football had been such an important part of Armani's life, he often found himself using a lot of football analogies. They came to him so naturally because he found that football and business had a lot in common. For him, breaking down film for an opponent was similar to analyzing a market; repetitiously practicing plays was similar to having frequent status meetings with the design teams; making a touchdown was similar to finally getting an account signed; and gaining spikes was winning the Super Bowl.

Armani looked at his watch and it was 5:45 p.m. He didn't want to but, he knew that it was past time to pack things up and pick up his daughter. Given the time, he knew that he was going to be about thirty minutes late. Since he would be traveling in Atlanta traffic, on a Friday, he added another twenty minutes to that time.

The day care was a stickler for promptness. Armani understood this and realized that, if he had been with screaming kids all day, he would want the parents to be on time, too. Armani knew he probably would have to pay a fifty-dollar fee. However, he had no intention of paying the penalty. He intended for Shelia to pay the late fee out her funds because she had called him at the last minute to pick up Sierra.

Shelia had just made it to the restaurant to meet Tonya when she heard the voices in her head speaking. (Still Small Voice: "Shelia, you are beginning to walk in pride." Loud Voice: "Girl, if you got it, flaunt it!") As she entered the restaurant, Shelia became aware of the attention that she was receiving from the men at the bar. In response to their eyes following her, she lowered her head and gazed at the floor.

Periodically, Shelia would intentionally look down to humble herself. She did not want to appear arrogant by seeming to carry herself as if she was all that. Shelia, not being a self-consumed person, sometimes forgot how much attention she often drew as a beautiful woman. It was because she had a J-Lo type figure and legs that seemed to go on for days. She held her hand around her waist to meet her purse in an attempt to hide her only defect, the pouch around her mid-section.

Despite her beauty, Shelia was not vain, though her good looks had manifested when she was a very young lady. She was such a strikingly beautiful child that her parents allowed her to model some in grade school. However, being more concerned about her getting a good education than about her pursuing a modeling career, they pulled her out of the modeling game. As she grew older, Shelia's interests in modeling faded, especially when she realized how much she enjoyed eating.

Glancing around the room, Shelia spotted Tonya waving wildly to her from a corner of the restaurant. Excited about seeing Tonya, Shelia rushed over to the seat where her friend was located. In her hurry, focusing on Tonya smiling at her, Shelia tripped over her own feet as she rushed towards the table. Tonya, laughing at her clumsy girlfriend, got up and pulled a chair out for Shelia, and said "Girl, for a moment there I thought I would be picking you up!" Laughing at herself, Shelia replied, "Girl, I thought so too...and I haven't even had my first drink!!" Frowning, with her head titled to side, Tonya looked at Shelia and said, "I can't tell. You sure you didn't have one before you got here?" Then they both burst out with laughters.

Shelia sat down and turned her chair so that she could sit closer to Tonya, who leaned in and asked, "So what's going on?" Shelia, still smiling, paused, then took a deep breath and said, "Armani, girl." Tonya looked at Shelia and appeared agitated. Then she asked, "Is he cheating again? I done told you to leave his sorry no-good A*S!!! You didn't sign no Pre-nup!"

Tonya's voice faded as Shelia looked at her, having no expression on her face. As she blankly stared at Tonya, she thought, "Tonya is an educated woman, but she can really be ghetto when she's upset...." Shelia interrupted Tonya's tirade and replied, "No, he's not cheating...Well... I think he might be...I mean I don't know...I mean... That's not why I'm here." Looking around the room, Shelia said, "Where is the waiter? I need a drink...I really don't know what Armani's doing. He's always working late." As Shelia was about to continue her explanation to Tonya, the waiter returned and interrupted, hurriedly asking, "What can I get you to drink?"

Shelia looked at the menu and then asked Tonya, "So what are you drinking?" Tonya answered, "A Texas margarita." Shelia stated to the waiter, "I'll have that as well." The waiter jotted something on his pad and then asked, "Would you ladies like to order or would you like a little more time?" Shelia replied, "Give us a minute, please." Tonya nodded in agreement. Tonya picked

up her drink and took a sip. Looking at Shelia with anticipation, she said, "Go on, girl." Shelia began, "Well, it's not
like he's really changed, but I feel like we just don't have
the same connection that we used to. It's like there is a
stranger in my house. Pausing and breathing, she said, I
feel like I'm in the marriage all by myself."

Taking another sip of her drink and thinking to herself, "I bet he's cheating!" Tonya asked, "So what do you
think is the problem?" Shelia began pouring her heart out.
"I don't know. We go to work; I come home; he comes
home, usually late; and he's very distant. We hardly have
sex, let alone "make love" anymore and I just feel like…
All I can say is that I just feel like I'm in this marriage by
myself.…"

Sympathetically, Tonya said, "Mmm…hmmm…and
asked, "Well, have you thought about counseling?" Shelia
replied, "I wonder if Mani would agree to participate in
counseling." Tonya reached out and patted Shelia's hand
and said, "I wasn't talking about Armani going to counseling. I was talking about you going to counseling."
Shelia, looking at Tonya with mild amazement, responded,
"You know, I never thought about doing that…You mean
by myself." Tonya sat, sipping her drink, with her head
cocked to slightly to the left. She was smiling and looking
at Shelia. Shelia was thinking to herself, "Now I see why
Tonya and I hit it off so well. She's a wise little cookie."
Shelia began to nod her head and said to Tonya, "You
know, I'll think about it…but right now the bartender is
going to be my counselor. Where is that waiter!?" They
both erupted in laughter and gave each other a high five.

CHAPTER 4

PRIORITIES

Dexter Lewis lifted the garage door with his remote and noticed that his wife's car was not in its normal spot, which brought a small smile to the corner of his mouth. He realized that Helen was either working late, stuck in traffic, or both. It did not really matter to him why she was not home, her not being there meant that he had the house all to himself.

Helen's absence when he got home made him smile. It made him think back on times when his marriage was good, when he could not wait to get home to Helen, and when she was just as eager to see him. Remembering an old song, he thought to himself, "Teddy was right. Love is so good, loving somebody, when that somebody loves you back."

Pensively, Dexter shook his head as he wondered about what happened to the happiness that he and Helen had once shared. He thought, "I guess life happened." Among the numerous distractions in Dexter's life that no doubt impacted his and Helen's marriage. He thought of the grind of coaching, the schedule of countless games, the late practices, and seemingly endless "parent complaining sessions," as he called them. He then shook his head and muttered, "I must face my own mirror."

After letting the garage door back down, Dexter found himself standing in the spot where

Helen parked her car. As he stood there staring in the empty spot, he realized, regretfully, that he and Helen were the main reasons that their marriage had deteriorated. They had stopped spending time with each other. They had stopped enjoying each other, they stopped having fun together. They had allowed the day-to-day grind of life to steal the fun out of their marriage. It's the simple things in relationship that keep the magic he thought.

Dexter walked from the garage into the kitchen. He dropped his car keys on the glass table and placed the mail on the table. Dexter noted that the majority of it was bills, so he tossed them in the "in-coming" basket. Dexter really never cared for the "in" basket. However, Helen had insisted on having it so that she could track all of the bills. She had single-handedly decided that she would take over the bill paying. Dexter had agreed because he really did not mind, but also he wanted to keep the peace with Helen. So he dutifully did as she asked and purchased an "in-coming" basket for the mail.

Another reason that Dexter did not mind letting Helen handle the bills was that he was slightly amused by her enthusiasm and approach to bill paying. She loved watching and monitoring the flow of the money—especially the influx. She was absolutely inspired to keep on top of the bills and protect their credit the same way that a lioness would watch and protect her cubs.

Dexter left the kitchen and headed towards the bathroom in their bedroom. As he turned on hall towards his bedroom, he thought, "A hot shower will feel nice after shooting the ball around in the gym." He stripped down to his gym shorts, leaving a trail of sweaty gym clothes, his undershirt, and socks along the path into the bedroom. On the stereo in the bedroom, Dexter found the smooth jazz station, 87.2 FM, and momentarily swayed to the rhythms of the music by Eric Benet.

Relaxing to the music while listening with his eyes closed, he remembered that there was some Asti Spumante still in the refrigerator from last week. He decided that a glass of wine would be nice addition to his happy hour. He swayed into the kitchen, got the wine, and began to do slow dance on the way back to the bedroom. He took a sip of the wine, kicked off his boxers, and placed his glass on the night stand. He then went back in the bathroom, turn on the shower and adjusted the water temperature gauges. He then stepped into the shower. Grooving to the music playing in the background and enjoying the soothing shower, Dexter found himself in a joyful mood and started singing in the shower.

Having lost track of time and having been soothed and relaxed by the music and wine,
Dexter was jolted back to reality when he heard, "DEEE-EXXTER! DEEEEXXTEER MAURICE LEWIS! YOU HEAR ME CALLING YOU! DEEEXXTER!" Turning the water down slightly, Dexter screamed back, "WHAT!?!?" Helen resumed, "BOY, YOU HEAR ME CALLING YOU?!" Dexter, screaming over the water and the music, shouted, "WHAT??!! I'M IN THE SHOWER!" Dexter wondered to himself, "What now?"

In between all the screaming, Helen had begun to

stew. (Loud Voice in Helen's Head: "Look at these dishes in the sink. Look at his stank clothes on the floor! HOW DARE HE!" Still Small Voice: "It's just a little messy.") Helen entered the bedroom and shouted, "GET ALL THIS SH*T OFF THIS FLOOR…and WHO LEFT THE GLASS ON THE NIGHT STAND!?" Dexter turned his attention back to the soothing heat of the water in the shower. (Loud Voice in Dexter's Head: "That crazy b@#ch is on the war path again!" Still Small Voice: "Let it go.")

Dexter began mumbling, thinking to himself, "This chick is crazy. If we are the only two people that live in this house and she didn't leave the glass on the night stand, who else did she think left it?"

Having calmed down a bit, Helen started combing through the mail, thinking to herself,
"I've got to make sure that the Macy's bill goes out tomorrow…and the Visa bill by Monday to make sure that they are received before the due date." Feeling better after her tirade, Helen began to speak to Dexter over the music and the shower. (Loud Voice in Helen's Head: "Look, you need a break from this deadbeat and get with a real man! Tell him you have a home visit tonight!" Still Small Voice in Helen's Head: "That's a lie!") Helen, shouting over the noise of the shower, yelled: "I got a home visit tonight, dude!" Dexter, not really hearing her, shouted back: "UH HUH!" as if he had heard her.

It is easy for Helen to get away because sometimes she would do home visits as spot checks on the foster parents of the children for whom she was the primary caseworker. As a supervisor, she was no longer required to conduct home visits. But Dexter would not have known that.

Helen stood in her closet and thought, "What should I wear? The outfit can't be too sexy because Dexter will suspect something." (Loud Voice in Helen's Head: "Let him have it about the grass soon as he gets his sorry A*S out of the shower." Still Small Voice: "It's just grass.") Then she thought, "I don't want anything too business-like; I want to keep it casual. Mr. Wilkes is fine, but he is not fine enough for a dress on a Monday."

Helen thought about a moment from her childhood and smiled when she realized where she had heard that statement before. Her mother used to say that about her father back when they were dating. Reminiscing, she recalled her mother saying, "Child, he was fine enough to make me wear a dress on a Monday, that's how fine he was!"

Dexter finished his shower, turned the water off, and shouted, "Hey, babe!"…but got no answer. While drying off with a towel he said, "I was thinking we could catch a movie later?" Still not receiving an answer from Helen, he started walking into the closet to see if she had heard him. Seeing her there, Dexter repeated his inquiry while drying off his legs, "I thought we'd take in a movie tonight." Helen coldly responded, "Well, you thought wrong. I just told you, I have a home visit and I'm not sure how long this visit will take and besides," raising her voice, "The only movie you need to be watching is The Great Grass-by!"

Dexter, smiling slightly, thought that Helen's quip was quite witty and remembered that she could be very comical when she wanted to be. Dexter replied, "I will cut it tomorrow!" (Loud Voice in Dexter's Head: "F@#$k the grass!" Still Small Voice in Dexter's Head: "You just gave your word.") Helen continued, "The grass is all up on the sidewalk. Have you noticed how nice Jeanie Smith's husband keeps their yard?"

Dexter thought, "Smith should keep his yard up—after all, he's retired and that's all he thinks about anyway…how to cut the grass in the right direction, how to edge their yard, and what type of grass grows better in the Houston summer heat." This was the reason why Dexter never rushed over to speak to him when he did see him in the yard. It seems that old guys love telling people what to do. (Loud Voice in Dexter's Head: "Tell her to cut the D*MN grass herself!" Still Small Voice in Dexter's Head: "Smile and let it go.")

Dexter, now looking her in the eyes, said, "If cutting the grass is that important to you, why don't you cut it?" Helen gave him a look as if to say, "Don't make me slap you!"

Dexter knew that Helen would not cut the grass because she had very severe allergies. The condition was so bad that at times—especially during the spring—she had to take antibiotic shots to alleviate the related headaches, sneezing, and congestion. He also knew that she was too prissy and lazy to do any work around, inside, or outside of the house. But she would complain about how dirty the house was and how the grass was not kept.

Helen was selecting a pair of blue jeans and moving Dexter slightly out of her way to go into the bathroom.

(Loud Voice in Helen's Head: "Ignorant A*S NEGRO."
Still Small Voice in Helen's Head: Silence.) After a few
moments of silence, Helen began speaking to Dexter and
then she sternly said, "Look Lil Man… I know you don't
understand property value, since you and your momma
grew up in the woods, but we live in a community that is
governed by a homeowners association. They formed this
group because of ignorant A*S Negroes like yourself, who
don't have the good sense God gave them to understand
that if you don't keep your property up, it loses its value.
It's a shame to look out the window and see my property
value floating away!"

Dexter was frowning now. He wasn't angry about
the ignorant reference. It was the Lil
Man comment Helen had uttered. He knew she was not
talking about his stature. She was referring to his penis size.
This was the comment that she used when she really
wanted to tick him off. Helen had made no negative comments about the size of his penis when they were dating. He
recalled that she seemed very pleased, back then. The critical comments first came during a heated argument when
she shouted to him that she had never dated a man with
such a small penis and that sometimes it was difficult for
her to feel him inside of her. Helen had lied, but she had intended to hurt him and she succeeded.

By this point, Dexter was livid. He dressed quickly,
stormed out of the room, and began looking for his car
keys. Helen, speaking loudly for him to hear her in the
other room, shouted: "There you go again, Lil Man, running away from your problems, instead of facing them. Just

like a momma's boy."

(Loud Voice in Dexter's Head: "How is she going to call you 'Lil Man' in your own house!? CUSS HER OUT!" Still Small Voice in Dexter's Head: "Hold your Peace!") Dexter found his keys, but instead of leaving, he began walking around in little circles in the kitchen, trying to collect his thoughts. (Still Small Voice in Dexter's Head: "Take your time. It's not the end of the world." Loud Voice in Dexter's Head: "Yes is! This B@#$TCH just called you a 'little man' in your own house! Are you going to let her get away with that!?" Still Small Voice in Dexter's Head: "Forgive her. She doesn't know what she is doing.") Dexter stops pacing and then sighed heavily. He located his baseball cap and put it on, opened the garage door, and quickly pulled his Mazda out of the garage.

(Loud Voice in Helen's Head: "My plan worked perfectly. I knew the Lil Man comment would drive his broke A*S away." Still Small Voice: Silence.) Helen continued to dress, thinking, "I rarely pull the Lil Man card… and I only use it if it's absolutely necessary. Besides" she continued, "He should have cut the grass without my having to say anything about it in the first place. Men are so predictable. They are so caught up with the size of their penises. Men don't really get that sex begins outside of the bed, with consistent little hugs, and kisses. Small things have a big effect, first on a woman's heart and then her body."

Helen was lying when she told Dexter that all of the men she had been with before him had larger penises. She knew that Dexter's size was not the real issue. The real problem for Helen was that Dexter never made her feel appreciated and desired. She did not feel that there was ever any making love, cuddling, foreplay, or any type of affectionate touching. The whole act was over within a few short minutes. After she and Dexter had sex, she felt like a toilet in which Dexter dumped his semen. To make matters worse, when Dexter was finished, the Negro had nerve enough to just roll over and go to sleep. The roll over thing and his insensitivity had just completely turned her off her sexual feelings toward him.

Helen rationalized, "Women want to feel special to the men they share their lives and bodies with. But who's going to enlighten men on what women need? Who's going to hip them to the fact that, in order to really make love to a woman, a man needs to make love to her mind, as well as her body, and that it takes time to bring a woman's body in line with her mind?" As to her own needs, Helen never got the chance to get them met because by the time Helen got in the mood, Dexter's "needs had been met," and he had already rolled over and was soon snoring.
So she developed the Lil Man jab in an attempt to motivate him.

Helen turned around and looked in the mirror and said, "These size 12 jeans are fitting a little too snugly around these hips," she thought. "I'd better pull out my step aerobics tapes. This booty is a little too much for a size 12. Mr. Wilkes will be pleased though," she thought. Helen's reservations were for 8:00 p.m., and because it was just 6:30, she decided to take a long, soothing, hot bath. As she chuckled to herself, she thought, "A hot relaxing bath will help me get Lil Man off my mind."

While driving, Dexter was distracted and was not really sure of where he was heading. He just wanted to clear his mind and get away from the B@#TCH at home. (Still Small Voice in Dexter's Head: "Calm down. Just calm down." Loud Voice in Dexter's Head: "Calm DOWN HELL! This B@#TCH just called you a Lil Man in your own house! If you let her get away with that, you are a lil man! Punk A*s!") He remembered a billboard sign that quoted divorce rates at $499 and he wondered if this was the actual cost or a teaser rate. (Still Small Voice in Dexter's Head: "I hate divorces." Loud Voice in Dexter's Head: "Fool! You ain't got no marriage.")

Helen's Lil Man comment really hurt. Dexter then thought back when he would shower in the gym with the other players. He was not intentionally looking at other guys' bodies, but he did remember that some of his fellow seventh graders did have penises hanging half way down their legs it seemed. When Dexter noticed the differences between his penis and the other boys' he wondered, "When is mine going catch up to theirs?" He had certainly hoped that it would have happened by the time that he had gotten out of high school. It also hadn't helped that Dexter once happened to catch his brother coming out the shower and he realized that his penis was a lot smaller than Armani's.

The he thought, Helen never had an issue with the size of his penis while they were dating, but it seemed to be a problem for her now, after four years of marriage. The first time that Helen commented on his size, Dexter thought she was joking. But after she made the comment a few times, he realized that maybe she really thought he was too small.

Dexter was so disturbed by Helen's comments that he asked his doctor about what was an average penis size. His doctor told him he had a normal size penis and that whoever said otherwise was misinformed. Dexter was initially embarrassed to admit to his doctor that his wife had made the comments, but he did tell Helen what the doctor had said. Helen replied by asking, "What does a white doctor know about a black man's penis size?" Laughing, she said, "Of course to him it's normal because his winky is smaller than yours!" Helen's cruelty made Dexter even more upset, especially after hearing her sarcastic laugh.

Dexter ended up at Applebee's, but kept going because the parking lot was jammed full, which was usually the case on Friday nights. He decided to go to the Mexican place that was right next door. The restaurant had a nice bar where he could sit and just think and maybe have a drink or two. The bartender was Mexican, which was not a surprise since many people in Houston were Mexican or Tex-Mexican, as many of them liked to be called.

The bartender spoke with a half-Spanish, half-English accent or Spang-lish, as Dexter labeled it. "What's up, my brother? What are you having tonight?" Dexter did not object to being calling brother by a Mexican, since they had become labeled as the "new Negroes." He felt that he and the Mexicans where brothers, if nothing but brothers in spirit. "Jack and Coke, please," Dexter said. The bartender responded, "You got it, brother" and then he began to search for his Jack Daniel's.

Dexter really had come to his wit's end concerning his marriage. It was at times like these when he really missed his mother. Dexter, the younger of two boys, believed that he was his mother's favorite. His brother Armani was seven years older than he was and although he knew that his mother loved both of them, there was a special connection between him and his mother.

His mother would make him breakfast in the mornings and they would sit and talk with for hours. She was the one that had introduced him to his first cup of coffee. They both shared their hopes, dreams, and ideas that each had for their lives. His mother was a real talker. She could go on for hours, especially in the mornings. How he missed her. She had died of cancer before he finished high school.

Dexter and Armani never really got a chance to get to know their father, who was always away training, or so they were told. As a child, they thought of their father as this big prize fighter, another Muhammad Ali. Their father was tall and had an athletic build, like Armani. Dexter had taken his build after their mother, who was tall and slender.

As he got older, Dexter heard the rumors that when his father was supposed to have been off training, although he had not been. In reality, he was no more than a has-been and a washed-up, womanizing drunk. Dexter learned that his father had abused not only alcohol, but also crack cocaine.

Even having learned all that he had about his father's past, Dexter tried to hold on to the positive images that he had of him. However, he was finally forced to accept the ugly truth about his father's habits and lifestyle when he saw his father, for the he last time. This was at a family reunion in Detroit at an aunt's house. His father's looks were evidence of his hard life. The crack cocaine had really done a number on him. The previously big, husky man had been reduced to his size. Not only did he not look too kept-up, what Dexter's remember was the way he smelled,especially his breath.

When the bartender sat the Jack and Coke in front of him, Dexter snapped back to reality and nodded with approval and smiled. Though Dexter remained anxious, he was not so preoccupied that he did not notice the cute, young Mexican female sitting in the corner of the bar. (Still Small Voice in Dexter's Head: "She's just another attractive woman." Loud Voice in Dexter's Head: "WOW! She's a cutie and kind of sexy, with that long hair. Wonder if she's got any booty.") Dexter noticed how closely the bartender leaned in when he served the woman, and then thought, "She's probably his girlfriend," as he sipped his drink.

CHAPTER 5

SLIPPIN' AND TRIPPIN'

Armani looked apprehensively at his watch and then tried calling Shelia's cell phone again, only to hear his call go straight into her voicemail. (Still Small Voice in Armani's Head: "Just relax and calm down." Loud Voice: "Relax, hell. Leave her an angry message!") After his calls kept going to her voicemail, Armani realized that Shelia had pulled the old "bait and switch" move on him. She had called to say she had a meeting after work and asked him to pick up their daughter Sierra from the day care. Initially, he wanted to object to picking her up. However, because Shelia had promised to come home right after her meeting, he acquiesced.

Again, checking his watch and seeing the time, Armani was furious. He had already made a date with Martina and now he was home fixing a bowl of cereal for daughter. He really did not want to prepare anything major for her because he was hoping that Shelia would arrive soon. It was now 8:45 and Shelia had not arrived and was not answering her phone. Given the hour, Armani felt that he had no choice other than to call off his little rendezvous.

Armani dialed Martina's number. When she answered, he said, in a deep sexy voice, "Heeeey, baby girl. How you doing?" "Great!" Martina replied. Switching to a more business-like voice, Armani said, "Look, I've got some good news and some bad news." "Give me the good news first, Mani," Martina said. "Well, the good news is that my mind is there with you, but the bad news is my body is going to be on the other side of town." "Huh?" Martina questioned. Armani said, with disappointment in his voice, "I'm not going to be able to make it tonight. My wife thinks she's single." "Armani, what do you mean?" Martina asked. "Look, Tina, I'm just not going to be able to make it tonight," Armani snapped. Martina asked, in a puzzled tone, "So what's the problem Armani? Talk to me." Armani was getting even more frustrated and stated, sharply, to Martina, "Look I'm not going to make it tonight, dammit. Bye!"

Armani hung up the phone. He was furious by now and wondered to himself, "How could Shelia do this to me, making me stay at home with Sierra when she knew that I had Friday night plans. She's just being the queen B@#$TCH that she is." Coming back to himself, he thought about Sierra. She was being a little too quiet upstairs in her room. Sierra's bedroom was one of five in their spacious home. Given the distance from the upstairs to downstairs and to assure that Sierra heard him, Armani shouted loudly, "Sierra!" (pause) "SIERRA!" Sierra answered, "Yes, Father." Armani shook his head with displeasure as he thought about the fact that Shelia had taught Sierra to say Father, rather than Daddy, just as her parents had required her to address Shelia's father as Father.

Armani was not bothered by the fact that Sierra called him Father. In fact, he had no preference about being called Father, Daddy, Papa, or whatever. Since his father did not stay home much when he was growing up, titles did not play much of a part in their day-to-day lives. He and Dexter had not developed any particular moniker for their father. What did bother Armani was Shelia's insistence on the use of the word father as a required formality.

Getting closer to Sierra's room, Armani asked firmly, "What are you doing?" Sierra answered, "I'm watching television, Father." Armani replied, "Oh…Okay, baby. Go on and finish watching your program. Daddy…," Armani stammered, making a stumbling effort not to say Daddy then said, "Uhhh, Father was just making sure you were okay."

Sierra came out of her room, walked over to the stairway handrail, leaned forward, putting her head through the rail, and said, "I'm fine, Father." Then she asked, "When is Mother coming home?" Armani looked upward towards his daughter and said, "I don't know, baby, but don't you worry. Your daddy's home." Sierra, having been reassured, returned to her room skipping saying, "Okey, dokey."

Armani retrieved his Blackberry from the table, or his "crack-berry," as his brother Dexter would say, and di-aled Shelia's number. Once again, it went straight to her voicemail. (Loud Voice in Armani's Head: "CURSE!" Still Small Voice: "Don't curse.") Armani screamed, "F@#K!" and then slammed the Blackberry on the kitchen counter top. (Still Small Voice in Armani's Head: "Do something productive with your time." Loud Voice: "H@LL NO! Call her again, but this time curse her out!")

Armani looked at his watch again, sighed, and mumbled something under his breath. He then grabbed his laptop and went into the living room, an area he rarely entered. As he settled in on the overstuffed sofa, he began to track in his mind the events of the day regarding the Waterman account. He wanted to make sure that he could lower his bid by 25 percent, just in case his supervisor needed a lower account option.

Armani understood that showing up for work early was the easy part. The hard part was swimming with the sharks while at work. Every junior executive in the company was seeking an advantage and an opportunity to stand out among the competition. Armani knew that his best asset was one habit honed in from football, which was practice, practice, practice.

When it came to matching Armani's use of catchy ad phrases, the other junior executives never had a chance, especially when he used football terms to describe his concepts. Supervisors who heard Armani's pitches would smile and nod in agreement, appearing mesmerized and looking as though a light bulb of understanding had suddenly clicked on in their minds. Armani loved the admiration, the competition, the success—all of it!

Though Armani experienced great success with Lawson, he did not get it by just sitting on his rear end. He worked for it and he worked hard for it, using whatever resources were available to him. One resource that Armani had really come to love was the World Wide Web. In exploring the Web, Armani had come to realize that the Internet would provide a useful tool for advancing his business, first and then Lawson.

Not only did Armani believe that the Internet was

an incredible research aide, he also believed that placing ads there would be the future advertising trend. Others in the firm did not share his view but that did not daunt Armani, who was not afraid to think outside of the box in promoting himself and his accounts. In fact, he refused to even acknowledge that there was a proverbial box.

Armani had spent innumerable hours poring over Internet research in an effort to discover and uncover every marketing angle for the Waterman concept, which was a pet project of his. The stakes in winning the account were huge and Armani knew when it was assigned to him that he had received a fantastic opportunity to shine. He also knew that the success or failure of his pitch for the Waterman account could either break or propel his career.

Being the very confident person that he was, Armani was not overly concerned that his pitch for the Waterman account would fail. He believed that his "off-hook-thinking would prove to be a serious advantage over the other junior executives, who were more traditional thinkers and who did not want to take risks on accounts.

Armani's attention was drawn to the front door when he heard the rattling of keys. When he looked at the door, he saw Shelia gasp in reaction to seeing him sitting in the living room on the couch. The room was rarely occupied, especially by Armani. Shelia normally entered the house through the kitchen, from the garage. This time, however, she had entered a different way, presumably in an effort to try to sneak in and quickly go upstairs before Armani noticed her.

Armani, sitting in the dark, looked back at his laptop. Shelia, realizing that she had been caught, smiled and said, "Oh! Boy, you scared me." "What are you doing in here, Mani?" Armani never said a word. Seeing the look on his face, initially, Shelia was slightly nervous when he did not respond to her question. However, when she heard Sierra's voice gleefully shout, "Mother! Mother!" from the other room, she became instantly joyful and seemed to forget all about Armani and about the fact that he was upset with her."Heeeeey, sweetie!" Shelia said, while placing her car keys on the end table in the foyer. Shelia turned to pick Sierra up and gave her a loving embrace and kiss.

Armani looked up over his laptop and sternly snapped, "Where the hell have you been?" Shelia, pondering the question and Armani's tone, stated, "At a meeting, I told you." Sensing Armani's angry mood, she tried to diffuse the friction in the air by picking Sierra up in her arms and smiling while asking her, "So how was your day, sweetie?" Sierra smiled and said, "Oh Mother, let me tell you about Bobby today in school."

By now, Armani had become more agitated and asked more loudly, "WOMAN, where the HELL have you been?" Sierra, now realizing that another argument was on the horizon, seized the moment to play peacemaker and said out loud, "Oh! Oh! Mother, Father gave me some Cocoa Puffs for dinner and I ate them all up!"

Shelia, smiling to hide her agitation with Armani, responded to Sierra saying, "He did? Oh, that's great, sweetie. Your Father's 'coo coo' anyway, so Cocoa Puffs was a very good choice for a snack for him to feed you." Shelia, not wanting to argue in front of Sierra, placed her back on the floor and said, "Now go run your bath water and I will be up there shortly." Sierra, bouncing lightly, said, "Very well, Mother." and ran hurriedly up the spiral staircase.

Once Sierra had left the room, Armani began shouting at Shelia, with his fist clenched and waving in the air, looking up to the ceiling and demanding, "YOU HEARD ME, WOMAN! WHERE THE HELL HAVE YOU BEEN?!" Shelia remembered that her mother would handle hostile situations with her father by being quiet and polite, and simply replied, "After the meeting we went out."

"OUT WHERE?!?" Armani demanded loudly. "Oh, just to have drinks after my meeting," Shelia stated, with her mouth slightly twisted. "WITH WHO?... And I thought you had an office meeting????" Armani Shouted. (Still Small Voice in Shelia's Head: "Tell him the truth." Loud Voice: "That's not going to help. Keep the lie up.") Shelia, also shouting, replied loudly, "I DID HAVE A MEETING...THEN WE WENT FOR DRINKS!" Realizing that she was shouting, Shelia more calmly said, "The meeting spilled over to Café Morgan's in Buckhead." In her mind, she rationalized that what she had told Armani was not too bad because it was a half-truth.

Shelia did not really feel too badly about the lie that she had told Armani because she knew that there was only one reason he was upset. His temper was flared because she had thwarted his Friday night hoochie session. Though she needed a break and believed that she deserved one, she decided that she was not going to tell him anything. She had gone out just because she wanted to get away, to clear her mind and because she had figured out that he was indeed cheating.

Armani's ire really galled Shelia, given that he wanted to get out so he could go cheat. She looked at Armani with calm amazement and wondered why he didn't realize it did not take a rocket scientist to figure out that he was cheating and that his Friday night late sessions were really covers for booty calls.

Shelia really resented Armani telling her that he had late night working sessions, from which he returned home having a hint of a woman's perfume on his suits. She also resented the distance that she felt when she looked in his eyes. Even though she was deeply hurt and angry because of the cheating, Shelia loved Armani and did not want to leave him. No one made her feel the way that he did. She also did not want Sierra to be separated from her father.

Given that she had decided that she was not going to leave Armani, occasionally going out with her girlfriend Tonya gave Shelia some much needed relief. It gave her an opportunity to gather her thoughts and to just enjoy some girl talk. Tonya was glad to provide an outlet for Shelia. Tonya thought that Shelia needed more than a break and she had long wanted her to leave Armani. Shelia knew in heart that was too simple.

Even Tonya had to admit that Armani had been a good husband in the past, up until the time that Sierra was born. But the baby had added a few pounds around Shelia's midsection and it seemed to her that Armani's interest in his wife had waned after the birth. Shelia understood that men responded to visual stimuli, so she took it upon herself to hire a personal trainer to lose the extra weight, but it was a slow and tedious process…and it did not seem that Armani either noticed or even appreciated her efforts to make herself more attractive for him.

Shelia heard Armani shouting, "DO YOU HEAR ME WOMAN?" She snapped back to reality and again heard Armani's question that she had not yet answered. She asked, "Mani, why are you so upset?" "BECAUSE I HAD A MEETING TOO, AND YOU LEFT ME HERE TO BABYSIT YOUR CHILD!" Armani bellowed.

Shelia turned slowly and pondered his statement. "MY child?" she asked herself, but she did not allow his comment to upset her. She just wanted to give Sierra a bath and go to sleep. Besides, the Texas margaritas she had with Tonya were finally starting to take effect.

CHAPTER 6

TEMPTATION

Helen had just stepped away from her burgundy, late model Honda Accord when she noticed the parking attendant looking at her booty in her form fitting blue jeans. (Loud Voice in Helen's Head: "Twork that stuff, girl." Still Small Voice in Helen's Head: "You are walking in pride.") Helen had an attractive body and she knew how to "twork it," as they would say in the neighborhood where she grew up. Helen had a figure that would rival any video vixen and made many men wonder how she walked the way that she did. She was bowlegged and had a small waistline, which accentuated her ghetto booty, a term used by her girlfriends to describe her ample behind.

Helen was used to getting attention from the male species, so the attendant's gaze was nothing new to her. Not being daunted by men's attention, she did not feel compelled to return any attention that she received from men. However, in this case, Helen decided that she wanted the attendant's attention, so she took the ticket from the parking valet. Then she smiled, looked down, and stood back on her legs. After allowing the attendant to get a full, unencumbered view of her form, she turned and walked away, with a very lady-like yet seductive stride. The attendant paused and Helen thought, "I know you looking, playah. Enjoy!"

A couple exiting the restaurant moved aside as Helen approached the door, allowing her to enter. The gentleman paused and held the door for his wife and continued to hold the door for Helen. The wife smiled at Helen and then gave her husband a look that indicated, "Just open the door and that's it! Do not look back!" Being wise, the man smiled and was courteous, but looked only at his wife until she and Helen had gone through the door. Helen nodded to gesture, "Thank you," and entered the restaurant to find a smiling and waving Mr. Brandon Wilkes. (Loud Voice in Helen's Head: "Girl, ain't he just a cutie?" Still Small Voice: Silence.)

"Mr. Wilkes is smiling like a cat that had just found a block of cheese," Helen thought to herself. "Black men are so booty predictable. When a woman with an ample bottom comes into a room, they usually react like the proverbial deer caught in a car's headlights. They stop everything and stare, looking at you with big, dumb old smiles." Having completed her thought, Helen extended her hand to Mr. Wilkes, who greeted her very warmly, extending his hands towards her, with both palms facing up. Next, taking her right hand into both of his, Mr. Wilkes kissed the face of her hand in the middle.

Mr. Wilkes was wearing a very smart navy blue linen shirt, with khaki linen slacks. His shirt was tucked in so as to show off his 34-inch waistline, which accentuated his 48-inch muscular chest. Mr. Wilkes was an exercise fanatic. The result of his workouts was clearly visible when he left the top buttons of his shirts open to reveal the muscles rippling through his undershirt and the hair matted on his chest.

Mr. Brandon Wilkes had arrived at the restaurant early and had gotten them seats. (Loud Voice in Mr. Wilkes Head: "Boy, we are going to have fun with that! Don't blow it. Play it cool and take it slow. No need to hurry.") Mr. Wilkes said to Helen, "I've already gotten our seats…follow me." Helen, taking his lead, followed him to the table for two in the corner, thinking to herself, "Now, he's smooth."

Helen was uneasy about the whole thing and was thinking that, maybe, someone from work would see her, or maybe someone from the Lamar High School faculty, or maybe a student, or maybe… She stopped her mental wandering, as they arrived at their comfortable seats in the corner. To her delight, they were seated next to another black couple about their age. Helen acknowledged the other woman's presence by smiling before she sat down.

Looking around the restaurant, Helen thought, "The lighting is perfect—not too bright and not too soft." She did not want Mr. Wilkes to get the wrong idea. Mr. Wilkes motioned with his right hand for Helen to be seated first. She accepted his prompting and sat where he indicated.

The restaurant was an elegant seafood restaurant that had an upscale style. Helen took her cloth napkin off the table and placed it on her lap. The maître d', who had been following Mr. Wilkes, handed them each a menu. Helen reached in her purse to find her cell phone and to check whether Dexter had called. Mr. Wilkes sat down with his back towards the other diners and smiled. The waiter arrived and asked Helen if she wanted something to drink.

She smiled and answered yes. "It's Friday," she thought, "I could use a glass of Martell cognac." Helen asked the waiter for a Martell and Coke. The waiter made a note of Helen's order and looked inquiringly at Mr. Wilkes, who said, "Long Island Iced Tea."

After giving his order to the waiter, Mr. Wilkes thought to himself, "If anything does go down, I want to be ready." At the same time, Helen was thinking to herself, "I wonder if this makeup looks oily in this light?" Then she asked, "Where is the restroom?" Mr. Wilkes, having dined at the facility before, got up and gestured towards the front of the building. Helen slid from the booth, adjusted her top, and gave Mr. Wilkes — and perhaps all the other men who were watching as well—what they probably had been waiting for, the Helen Lewis "ho stroll"…the name that she gave to her sexy walk.

Mr. Wilkes heard the Loud Voice in his head say, "DAMN!" He then glanced around the room to see who else was watching the enchanting majesty of the Helen Lewis walk. Mr. Wilkes had spotted one guy in the corner that was looking at Helen. The look they exchanged indicated their agreement that "D@MN! SHE FINE!"

Mr. Wilkes took his seat and began to map out his strategy. He thought to himself,
"Okay, let's not blow this. Don't come on too pushy. Stand up when she returns from the restroom, open the car doors, look happy, smile, don't bring up sex, compliment her, don't bring up her husband, and ask about her day."

In the restroom, Helen was thinking to herself, "Mr. Wilkes can have a 'goodbye church hug' and that's it…and he will not be allowed to contact me for the next two days. You do not care how fine he is. You're a married woman and what's proper is proper." Helen finished adjusting her makeup then slipped her wedding ring into her purse, thinking, "Tonight, I wanna be free." After checking herself in the bathroom mirror, she returned to the table and, much to her surprise, found Mr. Wilkes standing to receive her.

Helen thought back for a moment to when she and Dexter were dating and remembered that Dexter used to do the same thing. Since they had been married, Helen could not remember the last time that Dexter had stood to receive her when she returned to a table. Nor could she remember the last time that they had gone out to dinner on a Friday night. The two of them had become an old married couple in just four years. "Wow!" she thought.

Mr. Wilkes brought Helen back to reality by asking, "So…how was your day?" Helen, perusing the menu, smiled and replied, "Oh, it was the usual. There were office reports, child attendance reports, and more phone calls being ignored," she said slightly laughing. Mr. Wilkes was also laughing.

Mr. Wilkes knew exactly what Helen meant by ignored phone calls because they had been talking about her job over the phone for the last month or so. During their conversations, Helen's usual complaint was that, as a social worker, it seemed to her as if no one actually ever spoke to anyone. He and Helen also discussed that most of her work was accomplished through voicemails and emails; that everyone seemed to be overworked; and that returning phone calls was not a priority, not even for Helen, a supervisor.

Helen looked intently at the menu. While trying to make a selection, she asked Mr.
Wilkes, if there was any news on a promotion that he was hoping to receive. Mr. Wilkes, whose eyes were sparkling, began telling her about the selection process of the United Parcel Service.

He also told her that he was really the only person that UPS could choose because he was the most qualified candidate for the position—the district manager's job—having been a supervisor for ten years. He admitted that he was particularly excited about the position because it would put him well above the six-figure salary range, which he considered to be quite an achievement for him as a black man who just turned forty.

The conversation between Helen and Brandon Wilkes was flowing. The music playing in the background provided the ultimate atmosphere for two friends enjoying each other's company on a Friday night. The restaurant where they were dining was located in the outskirts of the city of Houston. Their dining experience was excellent and Helen made a note to herself to return to the Shark Bar the next time that her family came to visit. She said to him, "Thank you, Mr. Wilkes you have been such a gentleman, I really enjoyed this evening."

Helen was really happy that she had allowed him to be her escort for the evening. When he paid the tab, Helen mentally added the cost of the lobster that he ordered, the shark that she had tried, plus their drinks, and estimated that the tab must have been in excess of $150. Additionally,

Mr. Wilkes tipped the parking valet for her, kissed her palm again, and closed her car door instead of allowing the parking attendant to do so. He motioned for her to roll down her window and said, "You may call me Brandon now." She said, "Okay, Mr. Brandon." He smiled and started shaking his head.

Helen really had enjoyed herself with Mr. Brandon Wilkes. He made her feel special. While driving home, she selected the preset R & B station on her car radio and allowed her mind to wonder about what it would be like to date Brandon.

Meanwhile at Papa Deux's, Dexter began to feel kind of buzzed because of the Jack and Coke that he had been sipping. The restaurant had begun to get crowded and as more patrons filled the bar area, now the bartender had gotten busy. Dexter noticed that the Mexican girl was still sitting at the bar, looking around the room, and sometimes glancing back at him. (Loud Voice in Dexter's Head: "Boy, you know she wants you." Still Small Voice: "Sit still. You are married.")

Dexter began wondering if his marriage was really over or whether this bump in the road would blow over. The problem was not just with Helen. He found his thoughts wandering to other women, especially the young lady at the dry cleaners. She was really not his type, but she was happy all the time and she always complimented him on his ties or his shoes. He knew that her compliments and kind gestures were, probably, only harmless flirtations. Yet, still he was drawn to the attention.

Though that young lady was not particularly his type, she really made him feel good about himself. She was chubby with a round face and a protruding midsection that she hid with her oversized black clothing. She had short hair, was dark-skinned, and had a tattoo on her right breast. Dexter pondered his impressions of her. (Loud Voice in Dexter's Head: "Bet she's got some big nipples." Still Small Voice: "You're heading into lust!")

No he thought, she's not the type of woman that would usually garner his attention. He liked light-skinned women with long hair, like Helen. But for some reason he found himself at work thinking about whether or not he should take some clothes to the cleaners.

The Mexican girl at the end of the bar looked past Dexter and their eyes met. Dexter focused on what the voices in his head were saying. (Loud Voice: "Oops! We caught her looking." Still Small Voice: "It was just a glance.") Dexter pretended not to see her looking and continued to glance around the room. He noticed couples lined against the wall and people leaning over each against each other at the bar trying to order drinks.

The mood in the restaurant was festive. The Friday night crowd really knew how to party. The men had smiles on their faces, the women were all dressed up, the atmosphere was light and bubbly, and everyone seemed happy— just because it was a Friday night in Houston, Texas.

Again, the Mexican girl glanced back at Dexter. Again, Dexter looked away. As he did, he heard the voices in his head speaking. (Loud Voice: "What do you need? A runway to land on, playa!?" Still Small Voice: "You are married!") Dexter began to wonder if the Mexican girl was the bartender's girl and if, maybe, she was looking at the bartender. Then his thoughts drifted back to Helen.

He felt that the romance in his and Helen's marriage was over. Their sex life—when Helen did grant him the privilege of having sex with her—was routine, at best. The real issue in his mind was fun. When did their marriage stop being fun? When did it become a business or social transaction?

They had the relationship like that of roommates. One of them paid the household bills and, at times, they may have shared the household chores. However, any personal interaction between them was kept to a minimum. (Loud Voice in Dexter's Head: "Why are you tripping on Helen when you have a Mexican hottie staring you in the face? Stop thinking and start flirting." Still Small Voice: "Take some time to think about your situation. Mull it over.")

Dexter looked again at the pretty Mexican girl sitting across from him at the bar. He noticed that she was not looking at him this time. She was speaking to the bartender. He drifted off into thought again and wondered, "Is marriage supposed to be fun all the time? Isn't it supposed to have ups and downs? Am I being too hasty and giving up on this marriage too soon, just because times have been a little rough lately?" Despite her mood swings, Helen has been a pretty good wife, so to speak. Also, Helen has many good assets: she keeps her hair and nails done, she keeps her body in shape, and she has good credit. Then he thought, "Our marriage could be better…but then again…it could be worse."

Dexter continued to ponder to himself, "Who has a perfect marriage anyway?" His mother and father surely had not. His father was constantly gone. Either he was on the road, boxing, womanizing, or doing a combination of activities. His mother was at home, saddled with the sole responsibility of raising him and his older brother, Armani. Dexter believed that his mother felt trapped and was prevented from going out and playing with the grown-ups, just like his father did.

His and Helen's marriage was stale and lifeless, and the only thing that Dexter felt he could do was stick it out. He thought, "What's the hurry to get a divorce?" It seemed to him that his entire circle of friends had rushed into separations and affairs every time things in their marriages became difficult. Sadly, it seemed as if his friends were looking for excuses to cheat. He, by contrast, was looking for every reason not to cheat.

Dexter's thoughts were interrupted by the voices conversing in his head. (Loud Voice: "Dude, check out the black chick who just sat down." Still Small Voice: "Check on your wife.")

Dexter looked at the clock on his cell phone and noticed that it was about 11:30 p.m. He realized that he had been away from the house for almost four hours. But for him, the time that he had spent away from home was well spent. His head was clearer and his thoughts were not as scrambled as they had been when he left home. Concerning Helen, the real issue to him was commitment. He realized that he was in the marriage for the long haul, regardless of "the wall" that he and Helen were facing.

Despite the rough patches in his and Helen's marriage, Dexter knew that he did not get married to get divorced; he got married to give love. He really wanted his marriage to work and thought, "Why don't I apply the same principles to achieving success in this marriage that I used in coaching our famed championship game: "When the going gets tough, the man on the inside of you has to grow up."

CHAPTER 7

REVELATION OF SELF

Shelia lifted up her hands and loudly said, "Hallelujah!…Praise your Holy name Jesus!" With both hands lifted in the air, Shelia worshipped in the Spirit. (Still Small Voice: "Make a joyful noise unto the Lord." Loud Voice: Silence.)

When church was dismissed, Shelia thought to herself, "What are Sierra and I going to eat?" She started making her way through the crowd, reminding herself to smile because she did not want to be perceived as acting threatening or superior. Being a member of the church that she had joined proved interesting for Shelia because she, a white person, was a minority in the congregation.

At first, she was a bit uncomfortable. However, once she got over herself she learned two lessons. First, black people really were not so different than white people. Second, she had found that, if you treat them nicely and smile—for the most part— you reaped what you sowed. Shelia had to admit being outnumbered was different for her, but with a humble heart and a smile, she just decided that God would lead her towards the true Christians in the church. As she moved through her church family she made a mental note. She noticed that a lot people in the church don't even act like they know Christ. She could not help but wonder, "How could you know Him and not smile, in church?"

Shelia made her way towards the children's church portion of the sanctuary. She noticed that, for a Friday night, the church was pretty crowded. She thought, "These folks must be an outpouring of the anointing from the marriage and family series of sermons." Next, she pondered what her pastor had repeated over and over: "They who wait upon the Lord…He shall renew your strength." Sighing wearily, she thought, "I could use that some strength, given that Armani said that he's going to be late again tonight."

Shelia's mind drifted to Armani's being at home. These days, when he was home, he had only minimal interaction with her and even Sierra. But what troubled her in her spirit was that she could sense that something was weighing heavily on his heart. The word had informed her not to change the way she acted towards him. She got peace when she realized that changing Armani was the Lord's job and that her part was to wait on Him.

Each night Shelia prayed for Armani, asking, "Lord show him your Son and give him peace in his spirit." When Shelia would ask Armani what was troubling him, he would blame all of his frustration on work. She felt that he must be dealing with something much more pressing than that. Even though Shelia knew she had to wait on God to work on Armani, she also knew that she was not powerless in the meanwhile. The lessons on marriage and the family taught her that she was in a spiritual battle. She knew that as a wife, having a godly covenant with her husband, she had been granted the supernatural power to pray for her husband to be covered by the grace and protection of God.

The Word of God presented in the Bible had become real to Shelia and she learned to use it in her everyday life. She learned to worry less; and to lean not on her own understanding. She believed that if God promised it in his Word, it was up to Him to fulfill it. Armani had asked her once, "How do you know that you are going to heaven?" She picked up her bible and turned to John 3:16, and pointed and said emphatically, "It's in red that means it is based on the blood! God and I are under a contract!"

God's Word had become a source of comfort to Shelia. The Word gave her something else to focus on besides her troubles. It gave her hope for a better tomorrow. Also, the Word proved fruitful because the teachings helped her to smile and be patient, rather than to grumble and complain to Armani, as her girlfriend, Tonya, had suggested that she do.

By the time that Shelia arrived to get Sierra from her class, church may have ended but for the workers it probably was over by the time it started. This was evidenced by that frazzled look on the faces of the volunteers when Shelia poked her head though the door. Looking around the children's church, Shelia noticed that there were only a few volunteers and then reflected on the fact that she had done her shift last Sunday. Sympathizing with the weary, over-worked volunteers, she thought about a passage from a previous sermon and chuckled, thinking, "The laborers are truly few in children's church!"

Shelia touched Sierra on the nape of her neck as she played. Sierra gushed with a smile, turned, and laughed saying, "Mother, Mother!" holding up a book, "Did you hear about a guy named Daniel who played in the lions' den?" Shelia, laughing out loud, said, "I've heard about that guy named Daniel, but I'm sure he was not playing in the lions' den."

Sierra, speaking with bewilderment, replied, "But that's where I play Mother…in the den." Shelia was enjoying this playful banter with her child. However, looking at the faces of the volunteers, she knew they just wanted her to go play in her own den. Shelia smiled at the workers and looked for familiar faces, but she did not recognize anyone with whom she volunteered. In particular she was searching for the face of Mrs. Williams, who had been the one worker that made her feel welcome.

Shelia tried not to be offended by the way that some people at the church treated her because she found out most of the members really didn't know each other. She found that as a whole people were very polite, but aloof. Shelia had discovered some good news, however: The interaction through the service of others had broken down a barrier because the need was so great.

As to why they treated her impersonally, she didn't believe that her being white was the only issue. She also believed that she was being shunned because she was tall and quite beautiful. Shelia had gotten used to women observing her from afar at first, and then watching her to see if she was as attractive on the inside as she was on the outside.

Shelia had taken to Mrs. Williams because she did not seem to care how Shelia looked or whether she was white or black. It seemed most important to her that Shelia wanted to work in the ministry, so Mrs. Williams was just happy to have another pair of arms to hold the "crying gifts from God," as she would call them.

As they settled into the car, Shelia made sure that Sierra was fastened in her car seat and that the seat was properly secured. Then she looked in her purse for her cell phone so that she could call Armani. She thought that if he was coming home at a decent hour, he might want something to eat. She located the phone and hit the programmed button that dialed her husband.

The phone rang a couple of times then went to the voicemail. She thought to herself,
"Why do I even bother? He's not coming home early." She closed the phone and held back a tear, preventing it from welling up in her eye by shaking her head slowly. Shelia heard clearly in her mind a voice speak a scripture from a recent teaching: "The strong shall bear the infirmities of the weak."

Shelia turned on her radio and located a gospel station. She was hoping to find a song that would minister peace and comfort to her soul and alleviate the pain in her heart about her marriage. Shelia felt alone in her relationship with her husband. She could not understand why Armani could not see how much he was hurting her and how much she really loved him.

Shelia had now become aware of a voice, in her head, speaking to her: "I will never leave you, nor forsake you." While listening to the soothing music coming from the radio, Shelia began to smile, thinking to herself, "This too shall pass." Then she took a deep breath and turned around to check on Sierra, she notice that she fallen asleep holding her favorite rag-doll. Then she smiled.

Seeing Sierra sleeping so peacefully made Shelia smile again. She thought to herself,
"The real issues in life are simple—God, love, and family—and if the issues line up in the proper order, anything can be accomplished." Reflecting on God's priorities for family that she had been taught, she said out loud, "He might be cheating, but in our house we shall serve the Lord!" She decided she would maintain her love and devotion for him, in spite of the infidelity.

Shelia realized that she could not give up on Armani right now, and believed that the
God that she served would either restore their relationship or remove Armani from her life. The spirit of peace that spoke into her spirit comforted her in her decision to stand firm and preserve her marriage. (Still Small Voice: "I know the things that I have for you and they are good.")

Though Shelia heard a noisy voice in her head trying to discourage her (Loud Voice: "You know he ain't NO GOOD! His Daddy was No Good! You didn't sign a pre-nup!") Shelia decided that she would just ignore the Loud Voice, follow her Still Small Voice, and let God handle the details.

"I submit myself to God, I resist you Satan, now you must flee!" She said shaking her heading. She knew, in her heart, that she had only one choice. The series that her pastor had taught on the still small voice of God, informed her that, as a born again believer, she could evict the loud voice by speaking God words out loud.

*****

In another part of town

Armani pulled his black convertible Jaguar into the valet parking area of Charlotte's Supper Club. He looked up to see if there were any rain clouds and was glad to see that it was a very clear night. He looked in the rearview mirror and did a quick once-over of his hair to make sure that each strand was still in place. Having driven on the interstate with the top dropped, he did not want to lose his smooth.

Having completed his man-in-the-mirror routine, he stepped out of the Jaguar, putting on display his black alligator shoes. Armani's deep blue socks matched his navy blue, pinstriped slacks. He adjusted his tie and tossed the keys to the approaching parking attendant, instructing him, "Park it in the secure spot; I want to leave the top down." The parking attendant nodded, acknowledging the directions. Armani grabbed his suit jacket from the back seat and slid it on smoothly. The attendant handed Armani his valet ticket and Armani handed him a $50.00 bill. The attendant smiled and said, "I'll take real good care of her for you."

Armani smiled and re-adjusted his tie, then heard the voices in his head speaking. (Loud Voice: "Ain't nobody bad, like me." Still Small Voice: "Pride cometh before the fall.") Armani tilted his head slowly from the left to right to get the kinks out of his neck, which were there from his early morning workout. Hearing a pop, he began walking towards the entrance.

Armani had arrived at Charlotte's early in order to get good seats, before the Friday after-work crowd got too thick. He chose this spot because it was one of Atlanta's newest hangouts for the grown and sexy crowd. Also, he liked the layout of the club and the food was decent for the price.

Armani thought Charlotte's would be a perfect place to bring "the Toner," whom he wanted to impress with a business proposal. The Toner was in town on business, so Armani suggested that they meet for drinks before he caught his flight out of town later that night.

Armani had met Amani Toner during a rookie training camp, when Armani was trying to walk-on with the New York Giants. Toner immediately took a liking to Armani, based on the similarity of their names. Around camp, Amani called Armani his "little cousin." That connection was a big deal because, as a rookie trying to impress the coaches, any claim to fame was a help.

Even after Armani failed to make the camp, he stayed in touch with Toner. Whenever Armani was in New York, he and Toner would meet for lunch or dinner, just to discuss life, football, money, and of course the ladies. The latter were plentiful in Atlanta, or "The ATL" as many rappers called it. "The women-to-men ratio had to be at least 10:1," thought Armani. "When you factor in all the guys in jail, the gay, and the down low brothers, that number had to be at least 15:1."

Armani slipped the maître d' a $50.00 bill, hoping that it would allow him to walk past the crowd in the foyer, waiting to be seated. The man felt the crisp bill, looked at it, and saw that it was a fifty. He then looked at Armani, nodded, and said, "Right this way, sir."

Armani smiled and leaned slightly to his right in order to avoid hitting the elbow of a young lady standing in the lobby with a group of friends. The group in the foyer looked as if they did not approve of the VIP treatment Armani had just received. Armani listened to the voices in his head. (Loud Voice: "Money is a megaphone, baby!" Still Small Voice: Silence.)

All the women in the foyer seemed to be looking at Armani and he sensed the question from them, "Who is he?" Armani did not care. He had paid the price to be the boss and the maître d' volunteered to be his servant. Armani looked back at the young ladies and flashed his Madison Avenue smile. Several of the women smiled back at him and one started fanning herself. Armani thought, "With this tailored suit, this million dollar smile, and a hint of my Gucci cologne, sweetheart you don't have a chance." Again, Armani became aware of the voices speaking in his head. (Loud Voice: "Boy, You know you're fine!" Still Small Voice: Silence).

The maître d' escorted Armani to his seat and stepped back slightly and announced, "Here you are, sir. Patrice will be your server." He handed Armani a menu and asked, "Will you be dining alone or will there be a guest accompanying you?" Armani responded, "Yes. I'm expecting a guest. His name is Amani Toner."

The maître d' recognized the name and asked, "The Amani Toner of the New York Giants, sir?" Armani smiled and replied, "Yes. That's right." The maître d' assured him that he would personally escort Mr. Toner to the table. Then he dismissed himself.

As he waited, Armani thought about the idea he planned to present to his friend and what it might mean for his career. Armani had been with the Lawson Advertising Firm for five years and he was not looking to retiring from Lawson, or at anyone else's firm. He took advantage of every opportunity to learn the tricks of the trade that he would need to successfully launch his own agency.

Reflecting on his place with Lawson, Armani did not have that much confidence that he had a secure position there. He had determined that it would be just a matter of time before one of his accounts did not receive a spike from his ad campaign. That failure would be a chink in his armor and would probably result in his being cut from the team. Not wanting to be at the mercy of the advertising market and realizing that the field was crowed, Armani decided that he had better prepare for an alternative field. Just in case Lawson wanted to cut him from the "varsity team," in the same way that Denver had done drafting him.

Not only did Armani not want to be at the mercy of the advertising market, but he had also decided that he was not going to be the type of guy to whom you could hand a gold watch upon retirement. Just for making the Mount Rushmore office executives rich? Armani thought, "If any-one is going to be handing out gold watches, it's going to be me, giving watches to those who contribute to my reaching my own Mount Rushmore!"

When Armani invited Toner to join him for drinks, he did not mention the idea that he wanted pitch to him. Armani was convinced that the plan was innovative and beneficial for every NFL player. But he was not quite sure whether Toner could see the vision as he did.

Armani's idea was that, since each NFL player had a web page that was primarily constructed and controlled by the NFL, the players could all have their own private web blogs on which they could put their game day issues, training camp problems, and lifestyle blog notes. Additionally, the web page manager could count the number of hits that each blog received and market the number of hits to advertising companies such as Nike, Blockbuster Video, Toyota, as well as numerous others. The more popular the players would receive more hits.

Armani had his departure from Lawson all planned out. He envisioned that winning an ad account for someone like Toner would be the perfect launch for his own firm. Having his own company would assure that instead of his working for the Lawson executives, the executives would someday be working for him.

As a part of his plan, when he won Amani's ad account, Armani would hire someone to design and construct Toner's web page and to write the blog notes for Toner, if necessary.

All Toner had to do was concentrate on football and on playing well because the better he played, the more hits that Armani could sell for him.

Armani's thoughts about the pitch were disrupted by the waitress coming to the table. The waitress said, "Excuse me, sir. Can I get you something to drink?" Armani, being the perpetual flirt, said, "I don't know. Can you?" The waitress, seemingly in her mid-twenties, did not get the subtle jab at her grammar and cast Armani a puzzled look.

Armani smiled and said, "Yes, ma'am. I'll have a Jack and Coke." The waitress, a young, slim black woman with too much hair weave, repeated the order to Armani and seemed pleased at having remembered it correctly. She smiled, made a note on a pad, looked at Armani again, and then turned to leave. Armani watched her as she left, having lustful thoughts. (Loud Voice: "You know boy we haven't had a slim piece in a minute." Still Small Voice: Silence).

Armani found that the young lady had a very attractive figure, despite the bad weave, and the way she walked made his crotch tingle a bit. Armani's concentration on the waitress was broken as he gazed around the room. As he looked around, Armani thought, "There are some fine sisters up in here!" From his seat, Armani had a view that was slightly elevated, being able to see both the bar and the dance floor. He could see the women at the bar and they could see him. He caught one young lady looking back at him, but she lowered her gaze when she noticed that he had caught her looking at him.

The bar room game of cat-and-mouse reminded Armani of when he played tag in elementary school. Having matured since getting married, Armani had long since given up the bar scene. However, he thought that Toner would get a kick out of looking at all the fine ladies in the ATL.

Having grown wiser and wanting to protect his business reputation, Armani eventually realized that the bar scene had become too risky. Armani had come to believe that there were too many gold digging women in bars looking to "sleep up on" a better lifestyle. He also believed that, considering the onslaught of HIV—especially among black females in their 30s—"ho hopping" in the clubs was very unwise.

Also, for him, most of the women did not have much of a conversation and were not very career oriented. (Loud Voice: "You smell that? That's the smell of new coochie! Still Small Voice: "Silence.") Then he thought, On the other hand, one of the perks offered by the club was new screaming orgasms. Then he thought, this maybe what I need to take away this depression I feel? Just to keep his hunting skills sharpened, every now and again, he would go to the club. Then pick out the best looking young lady, and woo her till her underwear dropped off some time before the night ended.

Waiting for Amani, Armani thought, "Yes, pursuing a bar hit is risky business, but it can sure be fun!" Armani was distracting from scoping the club by the voices that he heard speaking in his head again. (Loud Voice: "Ask the waitress for her number." Still Small Voice: Silence).

CHAPTER 8

HOPES AND EXPECTATIONS

Dexter looked up at his dusty second-place trophy sitting on the top shelf of the bookcase in his office and thought to himself, "You might be having a little company." The phone call that he had just received brought a big-ole grin to his face. He had just talked with the basketball coach from the school where he used to work, Fairview Elementary. The coach informed him that Marcel Willis had just finished his course work for the summer and would be enrolling in Lamar High School in the fall.

This was the missing piece that Dexter had been looking for to complete his Hurricane offense. Marcel was only 5'5" but he had all the tools that Dexter was looking for in a point guard. The court speed that he possessed plus his ability to penetrate made him a natural to run his offense. Currently, in elementary school, he was making some mental mistakes on the court. However, Dexter believed that Marcel's ability to shoot over the defense would make up for any rookie mistakes he might currently be making.

Dexter knew that, with Marcel and with Darnel Smith, the sophomore big man he had on the inside, he could finally run the offense that took the team to the championship finals in his first year as coach. Yes, Dexter felt pretty good because he had found a way to incorporate "thunder and lightning" into strategic plan for his Hurricane offensive game plan. The speed and quickness and the out-side range was the lightning that Marcel would bring to the table. The defense would have to come out on the perimeter to guard against him. Then Marcel could pass the ball in the inside to Darnel, the thunder, who could easily get the big men on defense into foul trouble.

Dexter leaned back his chair and indulged in a fantasy, which he enjoyed until he became aware of the voices in his head. (Loud Voice: "The basketball god is smiling upon you. Now, you need to pray to the academic god and ask for this boy to get good grades in high school!" Still Small Voice: "There is only one true God.")

Still smiling at his victory he said, "This is going to be a great year. The basketball gods have smiled upon me!" Then he began thinking of all the work that he still needed to do before the practice season started. Though the players still had another month out for the summer, Dexter realized that he could not wait for the players to return before he began designing plays and looking at film from audacity to hope year.

Dexter had begun to envision Marcel and Darnel on the pick and roll. Then his office telephone rang and distracted him. Dexter picked up the phone, wondering who it could be. He answered and said, "Coach Lewis…He paused and said, Yes ma'am, I will be there right away." Dexter placed the handset back in the phone cradle and thought, "What could she possibly want with me?"

The phone call that interrupted his basketball fantasy was from Mrs. Shaw, the principal. As he was going to the office, Dexter was thinking, "I'm sure she wants me to fill in this summer for one of the teachers who can't make it in when school starts. Then again," he continued as he was walking to the office, "Maybe she wants me to fill in for the janitor this year."

Dexter sometimes filled in for teachers at the last minute to help out the faculty. He had completed some coursework at a junior college but had not obtained a degree. However when asked to fill in for teachers, he gladly said yes to Mrs. Shaw. He looked back one year and realized that he had filled for almost every teacher at the school— to include the English teacher, the Math teacher, and even the Biology teacher.

As he proceeded down the hall towards the main office, Dexter began hearing the voices in his head. (Loud Voice: "Aren't you going to call her out on the ring?" Still Small Voice: "Patience.") Dexter had not said anything to Helen when she returned home the other night. He had left the house after the argument they had, and returned to find her gone. To avoid any further confrontation that night, he pretended to be asleep and said nothing when she turned on the lights.

Dexter watched Helen as she started to undress. As she stepped out of her jeans, she stumbled and caught herself, with her left hand against the wall. That was when he noticed that her wedding ring was not on her finger. He never moved, so she thought he was asleep.

Though he said nothing then it bothered him, was she calling it quits he thought?

This was the first time that he ever seen Helen without her ring. She normally did not even remove it to take a shower. However, the next day, while she was sleeping, he looked at Helen's hand and saw that the ring was back on her finger. He shook his head and wondered, "Did I dream the whole thing or is Helen tipping out on me?" His mind was awash with speculations but that situation had to wait. He had arrived at the main office, knocked on the door, and awaited a response.

Mrs. Shaw and Dexter got along fine three years now, since he was selected as the new coach. He was a humble guy and did anything reasonable that Mrs. Shaw asked him to do. He really tried to fit in with the faculty and to be pleasant to be around. The fact that he was selected by the Board of Education, over her desires, initially had been a point of friction between the two of them. However, over time, the principal's opposition to his selection had begun to wane, especially as she discovered that Dexter was really a team player.

The faculty had also come around from its original position. At first, some members thought that Dexter would be arrogant because he had been brought in from outside their ranks. However, when he took the basketball team to the state finals, most of the gossip and hostilities ceased. The whole school and the surrounding community had come to be in his corner. At this point, he could do no wrong and the phrase, "Winning cures all ills" was certainly true in his case, at least in Dexter's mind.

Following his knock, Dexter heard Mrs. Shaw respond, "Come in." Dexter slowly opened the door, peeked in, and saw Mrs. Shaw at the copy machine. She was a heavy-set, stout woman, with dimples that made her look child-like when she smiled. She looked up and said, "Coach, go on in my office and take a seat. I will be right with you. I'm trying to make a few copies, since I don't have any administrative help here in the summer."

Dexter smiled and continued to walk into the office, thinking, "I'm probably here to make copies for her now." Dexter walked over to corner of her spacious office and sat in the last chair, on the far right, in front of her desk. Shortly afterwards, Mrs. Shaw came into the office and shut the door. She asked, "Coach, how are you doing?" Dexter's responded, "I'm fine, Mrs. Shaw. Things couldn't be better."

Mrs. Shaw walked past Dexter and moved a chair slightly so that she could navigate to her desk and could sit down. Dexter continued, "I got a call from Coach Hall, over at Fairview."

"Oh?" Mrs. Shaw interrupted. "Yes ma'am. Dexter continued excitedly, "Marcel passed his summer course work and will be able to enroll here this fall!"

Dexter was leaning back in his chair to see how the good news affected Mrs. Shaw, whose face lit up immediately. She recalled that Coach Lewis had kept her informed about the young man named Marcel, but she could not remember all the details surrounding his enrollment. With a student population of a thousand, it was hard for her to remember every detail about each student. But she recalled that Coach Lewis had an interest in this young man because he believed that the boy could help the basketball team met its "need for speed," whatever that meant.

Mrs. Shaw replied, "That's great, Coach. Now, the

reason that I've called you here is of even greater importance." Dexter adjusted his position in the chair, bracing himself, and fearing the worst. Mrs. Shaw handed him a brochure, folded three ways. Dexter accepted the brochure, scanned the front, and slightly opened the brochure to the middle section.

Mrs. Shaw said, "It's a coach's conference and I feel you have earned the right to attend this year." Dexter looked up, smiled, and said: "Thank you, Mrs. Shaw. This is great!" Mrs. Shaw continued, "It's at the Ritz-Carlton in Buckhead in Atlanta this year. Is that okay with you?" Dexter, grinning from ear to ear replied, "Yes ma'am!" Then he said, "I think this will help my coaching skills and play-calling." "That's pretty much what I thought when I came across the information on this conference," Mrs. Shaw said, smiling.

Dexter smiled as he reviewed the itinerary in the brochure. Mrs. Shaw stated, "Now you see that the conference is for almost a week and it's just a month or so away. Will that be a problem for you, regarding your early practice?" Dexter answered, "No ma'am. That's fine. Deacon Frye… Oops! I mean Coach Frye will be able to run the boys through the early drills."

Dexter had mistakenly referred to his assistant coach, William Frye, as Deacon because Coach Frye attended church regularly.

Dexter continued, "This conference will be an opportunity for me and my wife to have a mini-vacation. I have family in the area." Dexter made this comment to Mrs. Shaw, knowing all along that she knew of his brother in Atlanta, and that if it had not been for his brother, he may never have gotten the job at Lamar High School. Dexter, trying to get away from that touchy subject, stated, "Plus this will allow me to see what other coaches are doing and how to best utilize my players most effectively." Mrs. Shaw responded, "Very good, Coach. We really want to keep you motivated here and I felt this opportunity could only help."

*****

Helen's phone rang twice. She picked it up and, speaking into the receiver with a professional tone of voice, stated: "Ms. Lewis. May I help you?" A male voice responded, "I don't know. Can you?" Helen, recognizing the voice on the telephone, leaned back in her chair and began to smile. Losing her professional tone, she said pleasantly, "What are you doing, Mr. Wilkes…oh, I'm sorry, Brandon?" He replied, "Thinking about you." "Oh…really now?" Helen responded. Then, answering his question about what she was doing, she replied, "Oh, just working an abandonment issue, jotting down notes from a meeting, waiting for a response back from an attorney regarding custody…you know…the usual."

Brandon continued, "And that's why I called. I wanted to see if I could get you away from the usual so that we can celebrate." Helen asked excitedly, "Celebrate?!...Did you get the job!?" Brandon, grinning while speaking, "Yes ma'am, I did." Laughing, he said, "And I wanted you to be the first to know, aside from my accountant, of course!"

Helen cheered on Brandon, saying: "You go, boy! I'm very proud of you!! When did you find out?" Brandon answered, "Just now. I was called into a meeting and my director offered the position to me." Helen asked, "So what did you say?" Brandon responded, "I told him that I would think about the offer and would get back to him by Wednesday."

Helen was puzzled and asked, "Why did you say that when you knew all along that you wanted the position?" Brandon replied, "Because I wanted him to think that I had more than one iron in the fire." Helen responded, "...But you don't." Smiling, Brandon responded, "I know that, and you know that, but they don't know that!"

Helen, smiling, said, "I see. So you think you're pretty smooth, huh, Mr. Wilkes?"

Brandon answered, "Well, it's like Ray Charles once said, 'Umma make it do what it do, baby.'" Then they both laughed out loud.

Helen asked, "So, will this will mean a big raise?" Brandon responded, "Oh yes. I didn't get an MBA from Stanford for nothing. It's about time they really paid me. That's why I wanted to meet you for lunch. I'm thinking about selling my house. I've got a few real estate books, and I thought that maybe you could help me to review some things over lunch."

Helen wondered to herself, "Why would he want to sell his four-bedroom condo?" Then, snapping back to reality, Helen stated despondently, "Wow. Sounds like fun, kind sir. But I'm really in no position to break away right now.

I've been in meetings all morning and now I'm waiting for an attorney to call me back so that we can do a shelter move."

Brandon stated, "I feel you. Given that you are saving the world, the least I can do is be patient. Hey look, at least you know that I'm thinking about you and would like to have your company." Helen smiled and, feeling all warm inside, said, "Well, thank you for being patient. Now, get off my phone so that I can finish this report boy!" Brandon, smiling, replied, "Yes ma'am" and hung up the phone.

Helen became aware of the voices speaking in her head. (Loud Voice: "Now, this is a brother going somewhere." Still Small Voice: "You are already married to a brother who is already somewhere.") Helen placed the telephone receiver down, while the voices in her head engaged in a debate about the pros and cons of Dexter vs. Brandon. (Loud Voice: "Look girl...He's fine and rich. How many of this kind of man do you expect to come across your path? This may be an once-in-a-lifetime chance!" Still Small Voice: "Remember… for richer OR for poorer." Loud Voice: "You made a mistake. Admit it. Dexter is broke and boring and going nowhere!" Small Still Voice: "You took a vow.")

Helen shook herself, trying without success to silence internal voices that wouldn't stop.

Loud Voice: "People get divorced all the time. Let's face it; your relationship is dull."

Still Small Voice: "Marriage is what you make it."

Loud Voice: "Your marriage is horrible and your sex life STINKS."

Still Small Voice: "Remember… for better or for worse."

Loud Voice: "That stuff's in the movies. Look, you are young and beautiful. Why waste your best years on this sorry piece of a man?"

Still Small Voice: Silence.

Lost in her thoughts, Helen stood, glassy-eyed and transfixed as the debate between the voices continued to roll along.

Loud Voice: "Your relationship with Dexter has been over for years. You're living in a starter home. Brandon is moving into a mansion. DO THE MATH! It doesn't add up."

Still Small Voice: "You don't know that it's a mansion."

Loud Voice: "Why are you hanging on to a relationship that's not fulfilling?"

Still Small Voice: Silence.

Loud Voice: "Dexter is stale. All he talks about is sports. When was the last time he asked you how your day was?"

Still Small Voice: "When was the last time you asked him how HIS day was?"

Loud Voice: "He's got that little bitty pecker that doesn't stay hard half of the time."

Still Small Voice: What have you done to HELP him with that?"

Loud Voice: "Now, you KNOW Mr. Wilkes is packing by the size of his shoes!"

Still Small Voice: Silence.

Loud Voice: "You've been to counseling. What good has it done?"

Still Small Voice: "You've only been to counseling for a month…four times."

Loud Voice: "Let's be clear here. He's a momma's boy who can't even cut the grass." Still Small Voice: "It's just grass."

CHAPTER 9

BROTHAS

"What's up Smooth-Mo-D!?" Dexter animatedly stated into his cell phone. "What's going on, Hurricane?" Armani responded with the same enthusiasm as that shown by his brother. Dexter and Armani addressed each other by the nicknames that now had little relevance to anyone else, but when used in addressing each other, they were terms of endearment.

Dexter, speaking normally, asked, "Did I catch you at a bad time, big bro?" Armani replied, "No. It's cool, baby boy. I have a meeting in thirty minutes and I'm just going over some things. How have you been? How's Helen?" Dexter answered, "It's all good on this end. I'm calling because I received some good news and I wanted to talk to you about it." Armani, leaning up in his chair said, "Oh what's that?" Dexter, grinning, then said, "Helen and I will be in your city at the end of next month and I was hoping to see you then!"

Armani excitedly stated, "What! Get out! For what? Just a vacation?" Dexter answered,
"I guess you could call it that for Helen, but I'm scheduled for a coaches' conference. I will be in class all day, every day for like a week." Dexter continued hurriedly, "But Helen will be on a vacation. I'm sure her and Shelia will vacation in the malls!" Dexter laughed out loud.

Armani responded, "That's cool, baby boy. I'm really happy to hear that. You know you're welcome anytime here in Hot-lanta. We have plenty of room at the house." Dexter replied, "That won't be necessary, this time, bro. We will be staying at the Ritz-Carlton." Armani, smiling, asked, "What? The Ritz? What are they paying you over there?" Dexter answered, "Yeah man, the Ritz. I guess I must be doing something right!" Armani responded, "I guess that tournament run a few years back is paying off?" Dexter said, "It sure didn't hurt."

Dexter's tone began changing, reflecting the serious nature of the subject that he really wanted to discuss with his brother. Normally, their mother would be the one that he discussed the real issues of life with, but she had died some years past. Dexter really missed his mother. He began with, "Hey, Helen and I could use some time away, out of town." His tone became very somber. Then he said "See, our marriage has been kinda shaky lately." Armani sat back in his chair and checked his watch. Armani asked seriously while rocking back and forth, "Oh? What's been happening?"

Dexter, looking down, replied, "Well, it's just been kinda stale and we argue about the least little thing. We're just not happy." Armani really related to what Dexter was saying because he felt the same way about his own marriage. Dexter continued, "It's as if someone came in and just sucked the life out of our marriage." Armani lowered his head. Dexter said slowly, "Man, I can't explain it. Even after counseling, we do good for a while; then everything goes back to the normal stale relationship."

Armani's eyebrows rose as he asked, "Counseling? When did you guys start going to counseling?" Dexter answered, "I don't know, dude. Maybe, like…a month ago?" Armani was thinking that he could never go to counseling with Shelia for fear that it would get back at work. The rule at work was, "Never let them see your name in the funny papers."

Armani then asked, "Has it worked?" Dexter responded, "Well, yes and no. I mean…not really…I mean… we discuss things like what we don't like that the other one is doing or how better to communicate our feelings to one another. But it seems that, when we go back home, it's the same ole arguing…over nothing…really. I mean Helen nags and complains about the grass!"

Armani's attention drifted and he was thinking, "Well at least I don't have to deal with what's on his plate. Shelia is pretty pleasant most of the time." Then he wondered if the differences in Helen's and Shelia's personalities were a cultural thing, considering that Shelia was white and Helen was black.

Dexter continued, "I mean we argue over hair in the sink, what to watch on
TV, and even who drank the last orange juice. Can you believe that?" Armani was thinking that Dexter's and Helen's arguments were over some pretty petty stuff. Trying to change the mood and easing toward getting off the phone, Armani said, "Wow. Well, maybe this trip will be the little pick-me up for your relationship?"

Dexter answered, "Yeah bro. Maybe, but I'm really looking forward to coming to Atlanta because Duke's coach, Mike Krzyzewski, is supposed to be there. He's… like a mentor to me." Armani reflected back to when Dexter dreamed of attending Duke, but his basketball skills did not garner the looks of Duke or of any other big-time college ball programs. In fact,

Dexter barely got the junior college scholarship that he received. In the end, he might as well not have received the scholarship because he dropped out after he realized that he actually had to study and go to class.

In junior college, instead of going to class, Dexter would hang around the gym and play pick-up games with anyone willing, including elementary school kids. One day, when Dexter was playing around, a coach at the elementary school noticed Dexter teaching a student his crossover dribble and other ball-handling skills. The coach realized that Dexter had basketball instincts that he could actually convey to children. The coach was so impressed that he hired Dexter as his assistant.

Armani noticed the time and said, "Coach K, that should be cool, dude. So I guess you guys will have fun. But hey, little bro, I've got to run. Give Helen my best and I look forward to..." Dexter, interrupting said, "Hey Mani... the other reason I called is..." Armani braced himself, thinking that if Dexter called him Mani, he was going to ask for another loan, which would never be repaid. Armani said sharply, "Oh what's up?!"

Based on Armani's tone Dexter decided that this was not the time to ask for a loan continued, "I need you to pick me up from the airport. I mean they're paying for the flight and the hotel, but not for a rental car." Armani thought, "And you can't rent a car yourself?" But not wanting to pry into his brother's finances, he said, "Sure. Call my personal assistant and give her the details. I'll be happy to get you, little bro." Hearing Armani say, "personal assistant," Dexter thought, "Wow" and began to remember how important his big brother was to have a personal assistant.

Dexter knew in his heart that Armani would help him out because he was just like that. In Dexter's mind, Armani was always the star in the family. Physically, he was bigger than Dexter; he was also more popular, and the girls loved him. But despite all that, even though their mother praised Armani for his athletic skills, she had never made Dexter feel less special. In fact, Dexter believed that his mother went out of her way to make him feel that he was just as important to her as was Armani.

Armani was rich, good looking and popular, but that was okay with Dexter because, to him, he was just Armani, his big brother. They were seven years apart in age, but Armani did not treat Dexter as if he was a pesky little brother. In fact, Armani was really a good big brother.
He looked out for him in school, he protected him from the bullies, and, when he could, he even put in a good word to the coaches to try and get him more playing time. Dexter may have been the runt of the litter, but Armani did a lot of extra things to make him feel special.

Dexter realized that his brother had to go some important meeting and said, "Thanks, big bro. You're the best! Kiss Sierra and Shelia for me and we'll see you at the end of the month." Armani replied, "Alright. I shall…and you take care. Bye."

Armani placed the receiver back on the phone and thought, "I sure hope it works out with Cane and Helen."

Armani never really cared for Helen. From the start, he told Dexter that he thought Helen was a gold digger and that he was in over his head with her. But Dexter was so in love with Helen and that big ole booty of hers. When Dexter was looking at Helen's behind, no one could have told him anything. Helen, in Armani's mind, never loved his brother. Armani believed that Helen knew that Dexter was a good man who was stable and who had a decent job. However, he did not recall ever feeling that Helen appreciated Dexter for who he really was.

Armani recalled that Dexter had been coaching at the elementary school for two years when they met. To Armani, it seemed that Dexter's income from being an elementary basketball coach was never good enough and that Helen was always pushing him to make more money. It also seemed to him that, unless he was making six figures, Dexter would never be successful enough for Helen. Hoping that more money would bring a positive benefit to Dexter's marriage, Armani used his connections with the city's mayor to try and help his little brother to get an interview with Lamar High School.

Armani may have helped get Dexter an interview with the Board of Education and Administration of Lamar, but Dexter blew the board away with his basketball and coaching knowledge and his love for the kids. Still, the truth be known, had not Armani known the mayor from his college football days, the Board of Education probably would never have considered Dexter for the coaching job. Armani snapped back to reality and started going back over the tax extrapolations for the Wickham account.

Dexter, feeling happy after the phone conversation with Armani, decided that being in the office today was not fun anymore and that he wanted to get some lunch. He said to himself, "Why not invite my best girl?" He hit the pre-programmed button on his cellular phone and waited as the phone dialed Helen's number. The phone rang a couple of times; then he heard, "Ms. Lewis," as Helen shuffled papers. Dexter answered, "Don't you mean, Mrs. Lewis?" he asked, half smiling.

Helen did not really want to get into a long discussion about her title. She never used the moniker Mrs. Lewis at work. For some reason, the label was not something that she felt comfortable with. She had been working at the Department of Human Resources for three years before she met Dexter. From the time that she began working at DHR and even after they had gotten married, she had used Ms. when she answered the phone. Helen decided that there was no reason for her to change her title and that Dexter would just have to deal with it.

Helen dryly asked, "How can I help you?" Sensing that she was not in the mood for a challenge regarding the Ms. issue or for an accusation regarding the missing ring, Dexter decided not to aggravate Helen further and said, "No. The question is, 'How may I help you?'"

Helen was not trying to play his little games and said, "Uh, Dexter...What do you want?"

Dexter calmly replied, "I just wanted to know if I could take a beautiful lady to lunch?" Helen disinterestedly replied, "No, Dexter. You cannot. I have a deadline on a report and I have a child in a homeless shelter that I need to move."

Dexter began hearing voices in his head. (Loud Voice: "She's a B@#TCH!" Still

Small Voice: "Maybe she is busy.") Disappointed, Dexter stated, "Hey. I just wanted to get out of the office and grab something to eat and I just thought that maybe you wanted to come with me." Hearing the dejection in his voice, Helen humbled her tone and said, "Yeah. That would have been nice, but I'm swamped here. Maybe another time, okay?" Dexter quietly replied, "Yeah…maybe another time..." Then he remembered the good news that he had to tell her and he became excited.

"Hey babe, guess what I just found out?" Helen, hearing the excitement in his voice, asked, "What?" Dexter answered, "My boss just informed me that we will be attending a coaches' conference in Atlanta at the end of the month!" Helen, hearing "we," asked, "WE?"

Dexter, still excited, replied, "Yes. 'WE.' I want you to go with me. We can use the trip as an opportunity to rekindle our relationship. We can make the trip like a mini-honeymoon for us." Helen remembered that they had never really had a formal honeymoon, such as a cruise or an excursion to a resort island, because there was never any extra money for them to use to fund a real vacation. The money that they had been able to save, they used to purchase their home. Because they had depleted their entire savings, Helen knew that they could not afford to go to Atlanta. Having no money was the reason that she made an issue of "we" going to Atlanta.

Helen asked, "So where are we staying? I hope not

with your sell-out brother? Is the school paying for airline tickets for both of us?" The money Dexter was going to ask Armani for was for Helen to go shopping. Now realizing that the money for Helen's ticket had to come from somewhere, quickly suggested, "Well…no. But can't we scrape up enough money, from somewhere, to get you a ticket?"

Helen thought, "There he goes again, rushing out there without a clue as to how he's going to pay for something." Helen began, "Scrape up from where, Dexter? Buying the house exhausted all of our savings; our credit cards are maxed out from the new furniture that we bought; and I'm not about to sign for a loan to go on some coaches' trip with you."

The light bulb in Dexter's head popped on as an idea came to him and he asked, "What about asking your mother for the money? It can't be too much for a round-trip ticket to Atlanta." Helen raised and lowered her eyebrows raised them again and said sternly, "I'm not about to ask my mother for anything. We just paid her back the money that she loaned us to get the guest room furniture!"

Dexter sadly responded, "I just thought it would be a good idea for us to get away." Helen, tired of this moment with Mr. Broke, dryly said, "Well, think again and then think of how you plan to pay for your little getaway!" Sensing that Helen's mood was spiraling downward towards an argument, Dexter decided to let her go back to her work. Dexter said, "Well, hey…it was just a thought. Have a good day…Good bye". Helen answered, "Good bye."

After his conversation with Helen, Dexter's mood had changed. He was left wondering where the euphoric feeling he had possessed before the call to Helen had gone. He also wondered why Helen was able to so easily make him feel like crap.

Dexter sat in his office, staring at the ceiling, thinking, "All I want is just to get away with my wife. Is that so bad? Why does spending time, alone, with my own wife, have to be so difficult?" Even after Helen's heartless reaction about getting away with him, Dexter was not discouraged in his efforts to have his mini vacation with his wife. He promptly began thinking of other ways to get the money, including, maybe, pawning something. He thought, "It couldn't be that much for an airline ticket to Atlanta."

He knew Armani would come through for him on the shopping money. Although they had already borrowed the money needed for the down payment on Helen's new car loan, Dexter was certain that Armani would not mind helping them out again. In the midst of the flurry of thoughts flying around Dexter's head, he again became aware of the voices conversing there. (Loud Voice: "I don't know why you want her to go with you anyway." Still Small Voice: "Because she's your wife and getting away together couldn't do anything but help your marriage.")

CHAPTER 10

TO FORGIVE OR NOT TO FORGIVE

Shelia had fallen in love with her mini-mansion, the name that she had given to their new house, when she first laid eyes on it. She loved everything about the house, including the fact that it was a five-bedroom, off-white, stucco structure, with a spiral staircase that seemed to go on forever. She also loved the huge master bedroom suite, which was located downstairs.

Additionally, there were several other features about the house that Shelia loved, but what had really sold her on it was the orchard, which had a gazebo situated right in the middle of the spacious backyard. Shelia loved the orchard so because there she found peace and tranquility. She was able, without distractions, to kneel before God in her own Garden of Eden and to cry her heart out to Him, just as she was now doing. (Still Small Voice in Shelia's Head: "Jesus, Jesus, Jesus!" Loud Voice: Silence.)

Shelia had just finished another prayer for deliverance from her possible affliction. Her gynecologist had asked her to come back in for some additional tests because her Pap smear had revealed that there were an unusual amount of white corpuscles in her blood count. (Loud Voice in Shelia's Head: "Your cheating A@s husband has given you HIV." Small Voice: "Yea though I walk through the valley of the shadow of death.")

Shelia had been up since 3:30 a.m. in prayer before

the Lord, and now it was 5:30. She knew that Armani would be up soon. Standing in the orchard, she gazed across her expansive backyard towards the horizon, and noticed the morning sun beginning to peek over the tree limbs. Given the anomaly in the Pap smear, she knew she had to go get reexamined but she was not sure whether she should tell Armani.

Shelia asked herself, "What if it is nothing?" She did not want to tell her mother or
Tonya because of the conclusions that she knew they would jump derive. (Loud Voice in Shelia's Head: "You ought to go in there and wake his cheating A@S up!" Small Voice: "Cook your husband some breakfast.")

Shelia thinking to herself, "I want some pancakes." Then she began wondering in her mind, "where is the pancake frying pan in the cabinets? Then she thought, "I hope I've got enough cooking oil, because I sure don't feel like going to the store. She knew Armani would be up soon." Armani got up early on weekends just like any regular day in the week to work out. He then would have breakfast and read the whole time that he was eating, and then after eating, he would go to his office.

Armani was a consummate professional and he was religious about his work habits. He was so detailed in his actions that, by observing him, Shelia had actually learned good accounting habits as she watched him carefully check and double-check the accuracy of his reports. Shelia could definitely say this about her husband: though he might not be faithful in marriage, he was faithful to some things…his body and his career.

Shelia began to listen to the Still Small Voice speaking in her head: "The Lord is our Shepherd." Shelia's spiritual life had changed dramatically since she joined Globe Changers Church. There she learned about the two voices in her head from the pastor. She also learned that, if she practiced listening to the still small voice, she was following the voice of God. Additionally, she learned that the Loud Voice in her head was always negative, gloomy, and afraid. On the other hand, the Still Small Voice in her head was positive, upbeat, and hopeful. Moreover, she learned that the Word of God stifled and covered the noise made by the Loud Voice in one's mind, so that a listener can hear only the Still Small Voice of God.

Through practice, Shelia had found that the best time for her to listen for God's voice was in the early morning hours in the gazebo. Doing this first thing every morning set the tone for what she would do throughout her entire day. Leaving the gazebo, Shelia walked to the house and opened the back door. As she entered the house, she heard the familiar sound of the treadmill coming from the workout room. She knew that Armani was up, on time, like a time-driven machine.

Armani noticed an unusual amount of sweat on his towel, at the three-mile mark in his workout. He blamed it on the alcohol that he and Toner had drunk the night before at the club. In Armani's mind, last evening had gone well. The web-page pitch had gone as well as he could have expected. Toner listened, but Armani was not sure that he had heard details about the money he could make. Toner promised to have his agent call him and Armani was smart enough to let that be a yes for now. After the pitch, Armani and Toner began to party.

The bar scene in Atlanta was predictable. It was the same way it was in college, filled with girls that "do" and girls that "want to do." The girls that do could be spotted easily by their feet and their shoes. In Armani's experience, the girls that do usually wore cheap shoes and did not maintain them. Armani assessed the condition of a woman's shoes the way he assessed the condition of tires on a car: He determined that if a woman did not keep up her tires, she probably did not keep up her mind, her body, or her career.

Armani had found that, among the bar crowd, the girls that do would usually arrive looking "hungry" and would usually make it quite obvious that they were interested in you. On the other hand, the girls that "want to do" usually came to play hide and seek. Usually, their hair is laid; typically, their nails are done, especially their toenails; and frequently, they play cat-and-mouse games with their eyes.

On this night, while hanging with Toner, Armani was not cruising to get any phone numbers that he would probably have to throw away anyway. He came to play and the game was Amani Toner. Armani decided that he not come out to party; he had come out to run. He had made his pitch to Toner and now he would just let the evening flow. Armani believed that if he knew anything, he knew not to rush a sales pitch; that a patient runner always picked his own course or running spots; and that, sometimes, it was better to pause than to rush in.

The voices in Armani's head were already speaking to him as he started his day. (Still Small Voice: "Try to be happy." Loud Voice: "She better have breakfast ready!") Armani had just finished showering when he smelled the aroma of pancakes in the air. He grabbed his portfolio because he wanted to make sure to review his figures, again, for the Harris account. In particular, Armani wanted to make sure that the numbers for the second option that he might have to present had been extrapolated correctly concerning the out years. Armani also wanted to have a peaceful breakfast and planned to hide behind work, intending not to answer any questions about the time that he had gotten home last night.

Shelia, looking up after wiping oatmeal from Sierra's face, smiled and said, "Hey, babe."
Armani, trying to not smile, replied, "Heeey!" He then leaned over and kissed Sierra on her forehead and slammed the Harris file on the kitchen bar counter. Realizing that Armani was in a mood, Shelia said to him, "Do you need me and Pookie-Poo to get lost this afternoon?" Armani replied, "No. I'm cool. I have to go over a few more numbers and that will be it for me today." (Loud Voice in Armani's Head: "I hope this chick don't ask about last night." Still Small Voice: "She's your wife, not a chick!")

Shelia, sensing the opportunity to finally have a conversation with her husband, decided to be upbeat and hoped that, maybe, Armani would respond in kind. Because he had stated that he would be finishing up his work soon, Shelia decided that today might be a good time to ask him about the possibility of them going to marriage counseling.

Shelia was concerned about not approaching Armani at a bad time because she had learned, from watching her mother play her father like a fiddle, that there was a right way, and, most importantly, a right time to speak to a man about important matters.

Shelia smiled and told Sierra, "Rinse your plate off, Pookie, and put it in the dishwasher. Then wash up." Sierra asked Shelia, "Are we going shopping, Mother?" Shelia laughed and said, "Kind of. We are going to go shopping at the library. I'm looking for a dress that will fit your math size." Shelia and Armani were both laughing. However, Sierra was looking as if she did not get the joke and obediently jumped out of her chair, as instructed.

While Sierra was cleaning up herself, Shelia continued to clean the kitchen. Soon Shelia found herself singing along with the song playing in her head. Armani picked up the syrup and began looking for the butter, looking down as if he wanted to hide from his wife—or hide the shame that he may have felt because he was cheating on her. Armani sensed that something was up with Shelia because she did not bring up the fact that he had gotten in at 6:00 a.m. She was in a good mood and singing. He thought to himself, "Something is going on." Armani realized that it might be some time before he knew exactly what was going on with Shelia. Then he paused and said to himself, "She's been communicating with me differently since she began attending that church."

Most notably, since Shelia began going to Globe

Changers Church, when she became upset or angry, she no longer did her customary neck-roll thing, as if she had been influenced by watching too much BET. Now she just got quiet. Also, as far as Armani was aware, Shelia did not rummage through his clothes, through his brief case, or through his files trying to find evidence of his cheating. He determined this because he had planted a phone number in his briefcase to test whether Shelia was looking. Given that she had never mentioned the number, Armani just assumed that she had not looked through his things.

Shelia was not one who wore her religious convictions on her sleeve, but since she had been attending that church, Armani had noticed a night-and-day difference in how she handled and related to him. It was if Shelia was becoming a new creation right before his eyes. Shelia had asked Armani to go to church with her, but he said, "No thanks." For Armani, Sunday was truly a sacred day of rest and, on that day, the only church that Armani planned to practice was watching football religiously!

Shelia smiled at Armani and with gentleness said to him, "Hey babe, I've been thinking…" then she paused and looked into his eyes to see his response. Armani looked worriedly at Shelia. (Loud Voice in Armani's Head: "Here it comes!" Still Small Voice: Silence.) Shelia walked towards Armani, who was sitting at the kitchen table, stood back on her feet, cocked her head slightly, and gently asked, "Baby, do you think that we could use some marriage counseling?"

Armani, looking upset, replied, "Hell, NO, woman! I don't want no pastor telling me what 'thus said the Lord,' especially when he's not living it himself!" Armani then shoved his plate away from the table as if, all of sudden, he noticed that the food had a foul odor. He stormed out of the room, signaling the end of that conversation.

After storming out, Armani became aware of the voices speaking in his head. (Loud Voice: "Your Momma said that you can't trust white women! This B@#TCH is trying to get us fired! What if it gets back to the firm that your marriage is on the rocks?" Still Small Voice: Silence). Shelia, shocked and saddened by Armani's explosive reaction to the idea of counseling, closed her eyes, sighed deeply, sat down and began rubbing her temple with her right hand. In the quietness of the moment, she became aware of a voice speaking in her head saying "Jesus! Jesus! Jesus!"

<u>CHAPTER 11</u>

MISMATCHED AND DISCONTENTED

Three weeks later

Dexter had slipped into one of his trances that he would go into when Helen has had the floor for a while. This time, she was grandstanding in front of the marriage counselor. She was giving reason number seventy-eight… or was it the seventy-ninth reason why Dexter was an idiot?

To make matters worse, the marriage counselor was, in Dexter's mind, about as impartial as Helen's mother. She would seem to listen intently whenever Helen would speak while referring to the list she'd made of all the things he was doing wrong. From Dexter's perspective, there was little reason for him to even be in the counseling sessions because the doctor seemed to favor Helen's position. He would notice her frequently nodding at Helen when she spoke, as if to say, "Gone-girl."

Drifting, Dexter was thinking to himself that neither Helen nor the therapist had a clue as to why he had gone into shut-down mode in their marriage. It had nothing to do with his father not being home much, his lack of sensitivity, or his inability to tap into his feminine side. The real reason that he had withdrawn was because Helen had found that one emotional button that got to him—fear of inadequacy…of not measuring up as a man.

For Dexter, the straw that broke the camel's back

was Helen's revelation that not only was he lacking as a man, but now he did not even measure up in the bed. Now, whenever she wanted to really hurt him, all Helen had to do was say, "Little Man, come here." or "Lil Man, where are you going?" and without ever knowing it, she had uncovered his biggest weakness—his belief that he could not measure up as a man.

What Dexter could not understand was why Helen had not shown any signs of having any problem with his penis size while they were dating or after they got married. As far as Dexter was aware, Helen had just recently started having a problem with his "size" only about a month ago… at least that was when she started giving him an earful about him being a "lil man."

Helen, snapping her fingers in the air in Dexter's direction, said smartly, "Wake up, dude. Pay attention." The doctor asked you a question." (Loud Voice in Helen's Head: "There his punk A@S go, again, off in "la-la" land as usual!" Still Small Voice: "Be patient.") Coming back to attention, Dexter straightened up in his chair and asked, "Would you repeat the question?" The counselor replied, "Sure. What do you think is your reason for not wanting to have sex?" Dexter, sitting straight up, arched his back, smiled, and said: "Helen is the reason." Helen, looking shocked, leaned back in her chair and looked wide-eyed at Dexter, as did the counselor.

With all eyes on him, Dexter stood and, speaking with an elevated voice, said, "I get tired of her nagging, always find something wrong with everything I do." Dexter, half screaming, with his jaws clinched and his hands waiving in the air, continued shouting, "I can never please her! It's like every little thing I do is wrong!" (Loud Voice in Dexter's Head: "Give it to this heifer!" Still Small Voice: Silence.)

Breathing heavily and looking at Helen, Dexter said, "I can't live with that pressure, WOMAN!" Breathing slower and pausing, Dexter continued, "So I just shut down and stop doing anything around the house (hands waving in the air)…things like cutting the grass, keeping the cars up, and keeping you up in the bedroom." Dexter nodded his head at Helen and the counselor and sat back down.

(Loud Voice in Helen's Head: "This lil punk." Still Small Voice: "He's your husband.") Helen, rolling her eyes at Dexter, snapped her neck and said, "You weren't maintaining ALL THAT, Little Man." Then she turned her head away from Dexter and closed her eyes.

The counselor, sensing the tension, leaned over towards Dexter and asked softly, "Do you feel inadequate?" Dexter, leaned back in his chair, because he was astounded by the question and thought, "I know this chick ain't asking me this?!" He felt as if he had just whipped his penis out of his pants and had shown it to the counselor. Then the thought occurred to him that Helen must have listed it as an issue on her Intake Form under the section asking for the reason for their lack of intimacy.

After hearing the counselor's pointed question, Dexter was beyond frustrated. At a loss as to what to say or do now, he just shrugged his shoulders, sank in his chair, tilted his head upward, and began to cry. He had never really dealt with his latent feelings of inadequacy which made him feel guilty. Now, the guilt came down on him like a flood which had been held back for years.

Before now, he had never attributed his feelings of inadequacy to the size of his penis. His inadequacy was limited to only his physical size now and not what was in his pants.

He knew he had often felt that he did not measure up to Armani in most ways, including sports, speed, grades, or size. Though he had not always realized it, Dexter had come to understand that, growing up, he had been envious of Armani, especially when it came to size. Armani was bigger in stature, physically stronger and more financially established than Dexter, He felt the guilt and, at times over-whelming disappointment of not being an Armani-size man. For Dexter, his not measuring up to Armani was a failure that hurt him deeply. Yet, though he so desperately wanted to rise up to the bar that his brother had set, it seemed that no matter what he did, he could not do so. Now he was less than a man to the counselor.

Absorbed in the despair of his painful realizations, Dexter bent his head, placed it on his knees, and sobbed so deeply that the counselor ended the session. (Loud Voice in Helen's Head: "Yo lil punk A@S cost us our full session!" Still Small Voice: Silence.) Considering Dexter's mental state and his breakdown during the counseling session, Helen stated that she would drive them home. While driv-ing, Helen occupied herself with frequently checking her side and rearview mirrors as she changed lanes, maneuver-ing out of the Houston traffic.

The ride home was mostly silent until Helen, unable

to remain quiet any longer, looked over at Dexter, who was looking out of the window, and said with scorn, "So you know you cost us our money for a full session because of that little crying episode, Little Man…hmmm, don't you?!" Dexter continued to stare out of the window and said nothing. "You know my momma said you were a little momma's boy and she was right! Here you were crying like a little B@#$TCH boy who had pissed on himself in front of the counselor. What type of man are you? Stand up for yourself, Little Man! I'm through trying to make a boy into a MAN! I WANT OUT! I WANT A DIVORCE!"

Saying nothing, Dexter looked in Helen's direction and then turned back to the window, continuing to stare out of it. During Helen's ranting, she became aware of the voices speaking in her head. (Loud Voice: "Yeah, it's about time we got rid of this dead weight. He's been holding us down for years. It's time to be free and maybe date that cute Mr. Brandon Wilkes." Still Small Voice: Silence.)

After what seemed like an eternity, Helen and Dexter arrived at home. Helen pulled into the driveway, abruptly got out of the car, stomped into the house to the bedroom, and locked the door. Dexter got out of the car, still quiet. He entered the house, went into the great room, sat on the couch, and flipped on the TV to ESPN.

Though he and Helen had argued before, Dexter had been stunned into silence by Helen's actions and words because he had not see the D-word coming. Though they often argued, he and Helen had always found a way to resolve their conflicts. Until today, no one had ever opted to get out of the marriage.

Dexter sat silently wondering if, maybe, Helen's outburst had been made in the heat of their argument. He just could not believe that she could really want to leave him. Dexter was not deceived into believing that he and Helen had the perfect marriage, but he had always envisioned that his marriage would last forever.

When he thought of marriage, Dexter knew that he wanted one better than his parents had because though his father and mother were married, his father was never home. He wanted a marriage like the ones that he saw on TV, the ones where the husband and wife had a fun relationship. He wanted to be part of a happy, fun-loving couple. Dexter wondered what had happened to his and Helen's marriage to bring them to the point of discussing Divorce.

Reflecting on their current status, Dexter recalled that he and Helen had been happy during the early years of their marriage. They had one car and had fun just going to the mall to eat pizza. They laughed and played a lot back then, even when money was scarce.

He and Helen had always looked forward to advancing in their careers and making more money because they had assumed that more money would bring them more happiness.

However, now that they both had gained a measure of success in their careers, it seemed that the success and extra money had brought to them extra problems, not extra blessings. To Dexter, it seemed that the more money they made, the more plans that Helen made to spend it and no matter how much "it" was, "it" was never enough. Reflecting on Helen's increasing discontent, Dexter wondered, "What makes a woman happy anyway?"

After getting home, Helen had decided to take a relaxing bath. Stepping into the Jacuzzi tub, she rejoiced with at least one of the voices shouting in her head. (Loud Voice: "Free at last! Free at last! Thank God I'm free at last!" Still Small Voice: Silence.) She felt relieved as she reclined in the soothing tub. She felt as if a weight had been lifted off of her shoulders. Finally, she was getting rid of Dexter, the dead weight.

Helen admitted that she had wanted out of the marriage for some time. She could not say when her dissatisfaction had begun, but she knew that the sight of Dexter was starting to disgust her. Helen saw him as having no drive or professional aspirations for advancement. She felt that Dexter was comfortable being a high school coach and that such a life was fine with him. But Helen had decided that was not fine for her life.

When she got promoted to supervisor, Helen became the primary bread winner in the family. She resented that because she felt that, as a man who was making less than his wife, Dexter should have been motivated to seek a promotion or some type of career advancement. Instead of Dexter being motivated by her promotion, Helen felt that he became complacent and lazy.

As far as Helen could tell, Dexter was happy in their little starter home and had no aspirations for a better one, but this was not how she felt. Their current home was great, as a first home. However, Helen was ready for more. She wanted a brick house, not a house with brick facing and vinyl siding. Envisioning her dream house as she re-laxed in the Jacuzzi, she said to herself, "This time I want outdoor sprinklers, an in-ground swimming pool, a kitchen with an island sink in the center, and a fireplace in the mas-ter bedroom."

Helen felt that, at last, she had received her chance to be free from the bondage of her marriage to Dexter. She was very practical about the situation and reasoned that she deserved to be happy. Helen also concluded that she was still young and attractive and could remarry. "Next time," she thought, "Things will be different." She saw herself marrying a go-getter, a driven man, a man like Brandon Wilkes.

Under the influence of the relaxing and soothing bath, Helen acknowledged that she had married the wrong guy. As soon as she got to know Brandon she knew that he was the type of man she should have married. Helen saw him as being confident without being cocky. He was also an impeccable dresser and a self-motivated, driven brother. He was not some wimp momma's boy who could not get his penis out of his pants without instructions.

Sliding down in the Jacuzzi, Helen drew a deep breath and exhaled loudly. She said to herself, "I tried the counseling route. Counseling was Dexter's chance to really see where his faults were. But he never took any of it to heart. He never even tried to change." She laughed mock-ingly as she recalled the nickname that Armani frequently used to refer to Dexter. She thought, "This Cane certainly is not able!"

CHAPTER 12

JUST A FANTASY

Anna Marie had known Martina for at least three years from working with her at Bill and Buster's Restaurant. When she first noticed Martina, it was not because of her waitress skills or her beauty. It was the huge tips that Martina brought in that made Anna Marie stand up and take notice of her.

She noticed that as Martina approached customers, she complemented and bonded with the women first, not the men. She was making the women feel beautiful and special by complimenting their shoes, the style or color of their hair, or their makeup. Martina made the women melt like putty in her hands and, in turn, the women would make sure that she

got a nice tip—especially if the women had male companions to pay the tab. Anna Marie thought that Marina's maneuvers were shrewd, so she implemented some of her tactics. When she did, she found that she made better tips herself.

Anna Marie found it odd that, in all the years that she had worked with Martina, she had not heard Martina speak about a man…and certainly not in the way that she glowingly spoke of Mr. Armani Lewis. Before hearing Martina gush over him, Anna Marie thought Martina might have been bisexual. This Mister Lewis had Martina cooing like a school girl on her prom night. She would bring his name up in the conversion each time they talked. Though she understood that Martina thought that Mr. Lewis was a dreamboat, what Anna Marie could not understand was with all the single men in her age group, why was Martina so excited about a married man seven years her senior?

Having met Armani, Anna Marie thought he was decent looking, for a black man, and that he dressed nicely. But to Anna Marie, he was not all THAT. It was not just his looks that Anna Marie was lukewarm about; it was his being married.

Anna Marie's Catholic upbringing would not allow her to date a married man, to her, it was a sin. But Martina, who was not really religious, could not see why hooking up with a married man was a problem. She rationalized that, if Armani was happy at home, he would not have been tipping out on his wife or hitting on her.

Martina was sitting across from Anna Marie at the bar, thinking about what to discuss first with her. There were so many noisy thoughts rushing through her head, she was not sure where to start the conversation. (Loud Voice in Martina's Head: "Imagine yourself in that big house you saw in that magazine.") Anna Marie, seated at her favorite upscale tapas bar in Atlanta, began chewing her food slowly so that she could talk while eating. Martina and Anna Marie spoke to each other in Spanish to give themselves cover, just in case they wanted to people trash. In Spanish Martina said to Anna Marie, "Girl, I saw this kitchen today in this magazine." Snapping her fingers in the air, Martina continued, "It is to die for! It's got a fireplace in the kitchen that can be used as a grill oven! Can you believe that?"

Anna Marie was pushing the lettuce around in her salad while looking for a cherry tomato. She had endured just about enough of Martina's fantasy island and simply answered, "Humph...really?!" Receiving a less enthusiastic response than she expected, Martina asked, "So, what...like you're not going to want to cook on it when I get it?"

Anna Marie responded, "That's just it, Martina, how are you going to pay for a grill oven in your mansion on what we make at the restaurant?" Martina straightened her chair, as if she were about to do a catwalk strut and confidently stated, "Mani will take care of it for me." (Loud Voice in Anna Marie's Head: "This is one dizzy chick." Still Small Voice: Silence.)

Anna Marie, irritated by this time, cupped her hands to her mouth to simulate a shout and said, "Hello! He has a WIFE!" Martina sat back and said, "I know...He has one for now."

Anna Marie asked, "So has this man told you that he was leaving his wife and daughter?"
Martina responded, "Not in so many words." "Meaning he hasn't," Anna Marie stated. "Well, yes. He has. He's said it to me when I've felt his heart beating against my chest. He told me so, once, when he called me in the morning just to say hello. He told me again when he closed his eyes and kissed me gently. Oh, yes. He's told me."

Anna Marie shook her head, frowning, and angrily said, "You're delusional!" Martina playfully covered her ears and sang, "La...La...La...La...! I can't hear you. La... La... La." Then she began to laugh. Anna Marie pointed at her and said, "Trick, I done told you!" and laughed also.

Martina laughed outwardly, but the voices in her head were speaking to her about a subject that was not amusing. They reminded her of something that Anna Marie had said to her.

She told her that what she was doing with Armani was wrong, based on the teachings in the Bible, and that dating a married man was a sin. Anna Marie said God was displeased with her plans to marry a man who was already married to someone else. She also said that Martina was too pretty to settle for someone else's man. Then Anna Marie asked her, "How can you expect God's blessings on something that is sin from the start?"

At first, Martina blew off Anna Marie's cautions and concerns because she had never really cared about what God thought. Then she remember that one night, something happened in a dream. She saw herself falling into this huge burning lake, a lake of fire, and it startled her out of her sleep and left her in a cold sweat. When Martina awoke, she immediately began to cry. She got out of bed, stood in the mirror, and cried out, "Lord! GOD, I'M SORRY! GOD, I'M SORRY!" Then she got down on her knees and cried some more.

Reflecting on her relationship with Mani and on her dream, Martina felt dirty and sorrowful the remainder of the night, and had difficulty going to sleep. She never mentioned the dream or the experience to Anna Marie or to her mother because she was utterly afraid of what the dream meant. She just tried to put the whole thing out of her mind.

Martina's parents had never been religious while

she was growing up. Not having had much of a religious life carried over into her adulthood. She felt as if there was no Heaven or Hell and that whatever happened in her life happened, and that, after death, it was over. But, though the lake of fire dream was haunting her, she did her best to pretend that it was not bothering her.

Pondering Anna Marie's question about how she expected God to bless something that was not right, Martina became distracted by an invading voice in her head: "It's a myth! Hell does not exist!"

Martina, desperately seeking to change the topic of conversation, asked Anna Marie, "So what do you think about Pete?" "Pete who?" Anna Marie asked. "You know… Pete, the new waiter. Is he hot or what?" Anna Marie looked puzzled and wondered where Martina was going with this conversation. She answered, "I mean…he's okay. But he's kind of an airhead, don't you think?" Martina, looking off in the distance for moment, replied, "When we turn out the lights, I won't quiz him. OK?!" Then she burst out laughing. Anna Marie finally getting the joke burst into laughter also.

CHAPTER 13

HATE THE GAME, NOT THE PLAYA

Brandon Wilkes leaned back in his new office chair and reveled in the smell of new leather. He tried to determine whether the aroma was coming from the office chairs or from the plush sofa. Whatever the source was, he smiled and enjoyed the rich fragrance.

Brandon had just gotten the keys to his new house. He was particularly pleased with the deal that he got because the price that he paid for the house was now a steal. The seller was out of the country and the broker handling the deal made a rookie mistake. The price the broker quoted was not supposed to include the extra drapes and the window frames. The error cost the seller at least $8,000.

Right now, things were going so well for Brandon and that he said, "You know what Brandon? You the SH*T!" He felt that his life was heading in the right direction and that he was on track to accomplishing all of the goals that he had set for himself. Smiling and feeling full of himself, Brandon picked up the telephone and dialed a number. After a few rings, he heard the formal voice of a female sternly say, "This is Ms. Lewis." Brandon quickly said, "Hey lady. I know you are busy, but I wanted to know if we could do drinks after work. I want to show you something."

Helen was mildly surprised at the voice because she was expecting the caller to be one of her agents calling with another issue. Leaning back in her chair, she said, "That might be doable, Mr. Wilkes. Where are you talking about going?" Brandon replied, "Martini's, in Blount County. Is that cool?" Helen smiled and said, "Okay. But what is it that you have to show me?" Brandon using his deep voice said, "It's a surprise!"

*****

Later that afternoon

Brandon arrived at Martini's early to get a good seat. Being from the South Side of Chicago, he had learned that it was better to arrive early in order to avoid having to sit with your back to the door. The streets of Chicago had taught him one rule: "Don't be no fool. You can always get got! So don't leave your back exposed!"

It was exactly 6:00 p.m. when Brandon arrived. He entered the club and headed for a seat in the corner, adjacent to the door, so that he could see Helen arrive. (Loud Voice in Brandon's Head: "Imagine yourself tapping that big ole booty.") As he waited, Brandon looked around the supper club. There were not a lot of people there yet. However, he did see a few sisters who were looking his way. Because it was early, Brandon noticed the crowd to be sparse. That was a moot point to him because he did not plan on being in the club long. It was "triple 7" time for him.

He had played the little "Hee-Hee, Haw-Haw" game with Helen for six weeks now. They had been going to lunch and even dinner when Helen could get out, and all that he had to show for it was a sisterly hug and peck on his cheek. He decided that it was time for the "slot machine" to "pay out" or he was "cashing out."

Brandon reflected over his dating scheme, which he had adopted in college. His college fraternity had taught him the "three Fs" to dating: fool them, f@#k them, and forget them. He was already well on the way to accomplishing the first F with Helen and now he was working on accomplishing the second F.

Tonight, Brandon's surprise for Helen would begin with a tour of his new house. Following that would be a catered, candlelit dinner. There would also be lit candles all around the house, with a trail of them leading to his bedroom. He thought, "If the machine does not cash in tonight, the B@#TCH would be getting the "ole-Marty-Mart" treatment: 'Get ta Steppin!'" (Loud Voice in Brandon's Head: "Strokin it real slow from behind.") Looking at his watch, shaking his head, Brandon wondered how much time he would have to wait again. Helen was always late.

*****

In another part of town

Helen, stuck in traffic on the off ramp, looked into the mirror to make sure her lip stick did not need to be refreshed. She wondered to herself, "It's been six weeks and Brandon has been a total gentleman. What surprise could he possibly have for me? It's way too early for a ring, even

though he knows that Dexter and I are in the process of getting divorced. Well …he probably got me some flowers…
maybe some perfume…or maybe a scarf."

In the state of Texas, getting a divorce was a year-
long process. Helen determined that it would also take
about a year to get to know Brandon, so she thought it
would be wise for her to take her time and to really get to
know him before jumping into a serious relationship with
him. (Loud Voice in Helen's Head: "It's not adultery now!
You asked Dexter for a divorce! So you're free." Still Small
Voice: "But it is fornication!")

Helen was not someone who was quick to sleep
with a man—even if he was "fine as cat hair," as one of her
girlfriends described Brandon after seeing pictures of him.
She decided that, if Mr. Wilkes was not willing to wait, it
was his loss, not hers. Her body was not for sale, certainly
not for a lunch or a dinner that she could purchase for herself.

Helen finally cleared the Houston traffic and arrived
at the restaurant thirty minutes late. As she entered, Brandon stood as he saw her approach the foyer. Helen thought
to herself, "Why does he always get the corner seat, with
his back to wall?" She smiled at Brandon and gave him his
customary "church-hug." She then walked towards the
table he had selected. She strode confidently across the
room. Having come from work, Helen was dressed in business attire. Whether she wore business or casual clothes,
she carried herself with an air of confidence. Trying to
walk the way that saw her mother walk.

Helen thought it wise to try to maintain a business

air while in the restaurant. With that intention in mind, she surveyed the room to make sure that her little rendezvous was not being observed by any of her acquaintances who might leak damaging information back to Dexter.

She thought, "Even though Houston is a pretty large city, you can't ever be too careful."

Taking her seat, she noticed that Mr. Wilkes had taken the liberty of ordering her favorite cocktail. She adjusted her chair and said, "Thank you, kind sir." Brandon, smiling, held his sport jacket with this right hand so that the jacket would not be in the way as he sat down.

Gazing at Helen, Brandon realized that only the loud voice was speaking in his head. (Loud Voice: "Wonder what type underwear she's wearing under that business suit?") Having sat down, he said, "You look nice, baby girl, with your hair pulled back, all professional." Helen smiled then tasted her drink to make sure that it tasted like the usual. She responded, "Thank you. You look quite nice yourself, kind sir."

Brandon stayed with his script of asking Helen how her day had been and listening patiently as she gave him the highlights of being a supervisor at the Department of Human Resources. Then he ordered another round of drinks and asked about the divorce proceedings. Brandon now learned that Helen had filed the paperwork for the divorce and was waiting on Dexter to sign the house over to her and to move out. Helen also informed Brandon that Dexter had refused to sign the documents and wanted to continue counseling. Feeling cozy from the second round of drinks, Helen asked playfully, "So what's this surprise you have for me, Mr. Wilkes…My bad…Brandon?"

Brandon could hardly pay attention to Helen, being distracted by his own noisy thoughts. (Loud Voice in Brandon's Head: "Right here in my pants, sweetheart!") Brandon, seemingly caught off guard by Helen's question, slowly wiped his chin—as if to accentuate his reply—and said, "You're going to have to follow me to get it."

Helen sat up straight in the chair, arched her eyebrows, and asked, "FOLLOW YOU!

Follow you where playa!?" Then, Brandon, looking like a scared kid who had been caught leaving the refrigerator door open, answered hurriedly, "Well, it's not too far from here. I wanted to surprise you with catered seafood dinner at my new house." Brandon continued, holding his head down, "I just wanted you to see how blessed and highly favored I am." Helen, seemingly impressed with Brandon's use of scripture, responded, "Hmmmm….Oh Okay! Well, since it's not too far…I guess I could take a peek." (Loud Voice in Dexter's Head: "Whew! Dude, you almost blew it. Good use of that fake church SH*T!")

CHAPTER 14

IT'S A WRAP

Helen and Dexter had been living like roommates for past few weeks. On last Friday, Helen had come in after 3:00 a.m. for the first time in their marriage. Though Dexter was disturbed by her actions, he decided not to say anything. He did not want to get into a fight and he was not sure how much good it would do anyway. Hence, the past few weeks, there had not been very much conversation between them.

During this whole ordeal with his marriage, Dexter found that he really needed someone to talk with about what was going on in his life. Now he really missed his mother, but since she was not there, he reached out to the next best thing—his big brother, Armani. Armani knew that his brother was hurting so he took the time to regularly talk with him and to let his little brother get whatever was bothering him off his chest. Armani and Dexter had not always been as close as they had grown more recently. Now, they had gotten to the point where they communicated almost daily.

During one of their more recent conversations, Dexter told Armani about the deteriorating state of his marriage. Dexter tried to put a positive spin on the situation and revealed to Armani that at least he and Helen were having oral sex. Armani looked at his phone, frowning, and asked Dexter what he meant. Dexter answered, "We walk by each other and she says, 'SCREW YOU!' and I respond, 'SCREW YOU TOO!' Armani laughed, sensing that his brother must be really hurting.

Dexter had accepted that Helen was not going to Atlanta for the coach's conference, so he completed his travel plans for a solo trip. Now that this day had come for his scheduled departure to Atlanta, Dexter was packed and more than ready to go. He had made all of the necessary travel arrangements, and now he was waiting for Helen to take him to the airport.

He checked his luggage, once again, to make sure that he had enough memorabilia for Coach-K to sign in Atlanta at the conference. He wanted to impress the kids with at least a touch of greatness. He had already called the airline to make sure the flight to Atlanta was scheduled to depart from Houston on time. Having done all that he intended to do before he left, he sat with his arms folded in the kitchen to wait on Helen, again!

The coaches' conference was scheduled to last from Sunday through Thursday. However, He wanted to leave for Atlanta early on Saturday to get some long needed R&R. Just to spend some time with his big brother, his beautiful sister-in-law, and his lovely little niece "Ms. Sierra." He thought.

Dexter was mildly surprised, but thankful, that Helen agreed to take him to airport. To him, it did not make sense for him to leave his car parked at the airport, given the number of days that he would be gone. However, Dexter felt that Helen had only agreed to take him out of guilt for telling him that she wanted a divorce.

He had finally come to grips with the fact that his marriage was over. He and Armani had a long conversation. He was now at peace with signing the divorce papers. Armani had told him that he never really thought that Helen loved him. He thought she was just a gold digger. Armani said, in his opinion, the only reason Helen wanted him was because she wanted to ride the coattail. Their family had fame in Atlanta related to Armani's being an all-star at Georgia Tech and to Armani's having gone pro.

Then, Armani said something to Dexter that sounded like a comment that his mother would have made. He said, "She doesn't want you! Let her go!" And a light came on in his head and he felt a flood of peace for the first time about the divorce. Later that day he signed the papers.

In spite of everything that Armani had said to him, and everything that he had been through with Helen, Dexter still found himself thinking, "But why doesn't she want me? I want her." He just sat in the chair, holding his head down. Before he had a chance to get too depressed, he heard the garage door open.

Helen entered into the house holding the mail and tossed it on the kitchen table. She looked at Dexter, with his head down, and shouted abruptly, "I hope you're ready to go, Lil Man. I got to get back to work!" Though Helen's words bothered him, Dexter hardly reacted to the Lil-Man comment because, having heard it so much. It did not sting him the way that it used to. Dexter replied, "Yeah. I know. I'm all packed. Let's go." Then he said to Helen, "Check the "in-box." You'll find the divorce papers. I signed them. When I return, I'll be moving out."

Helen did not say anything out loud, but the voices in her head spoke out. (Loud Voice: "Hallelujah!" Still Small Voice: Silence.) Helen, slightly jarred by Dexter's news, stifled the smile that was trying to escape onto her face. She was especially pleased because she had thought that Dexter would drag the divorce out until at least the arbitration date, set for six months later.

Dexter's car was in the driveway. He noticed that Helen had already put her car in the garage, and then he thought, "She's probably driving my car to the airport." Dexter exited the house, walked over to his car, and placed his luggage in the car. While he was outside, Helen immediately went over the paperwork to see if he had given her the house. She found that he had given her the house, all of the furnishings, and the new Honda. Then, at the bottom of the paperwork, he had written on a sticky note, "I'm sorry you don't want me!"

As they were heading to the airport, Helen, feeling a bit remorseful about how ugly she had been to Dexter lately, said to him, "Dexter, thank you. It's truly for the best. We're both still young enough to find our soul mates." Dexter looked away through the mirror to see if her driving perception was correct for the traffic she had just entered. Then he looked at her.

Helen, sensing herself driving to slow to merge safely, sped up and entered into the Houston traffic heading towards the airport. The silence was awkward. After driving for some time, Helen sought something on the radio that was upbeat. As she adjusted the radio away from the R&B station to the urban hip-hop station, she asked Dexter,

"What time is your flight?" He answered dryly, "12:30."

While trying to focus on the road and feeling that she ought to say something to Dexter, Helen became aware of the voices that were disagreeing in her head. (Still Small Voice: "Apologize to him." Loud Voice: "You don't owe this loser anything.") She looked at the clock and eased up on the gas in order to avoid colliding with the merging traffic. She smiled and said to Dexter, "Look, Cane, this is for the best. You and I are on two different pages. You're ESPN and I'm Lifetime."

Dexter looked at Helen, becoming aware that she only used his nickname when she wanted something. He then began pointing towards the Delta Airlines sign to alert her to the upcoming turn. Making eye contact with Helen, he said, "I would have watched Lifetime with you!"

(Loud Voice in Helen's Head: "THAT'S NOT THE POINT, LIL MAN." Still Small Voice: Silence.) Helen, reflecting back to the early days of their marriage, recalled that, in fact, Dexter had watched Lifetime with her. She recalled one rainy Saturday morning when Dexter had cooked breakfast for her and served it to her in bed. Then they spent the rest of the day in bed with candles and popcorn, watching the Lifetime channel.

By the time that they pulled up to Delta's unloading zone, Dexter had gotten tired of the made-up small talk and bluntly stated, "Look, Helen, I would have done whatever you wanted me to do…and you know that. But for some reason unknown to me, you've decided that I am not what you want. I'm sorry that I can't be whoever it is that you want." Dexter, now tearing up slightly, opened the car door and said, "Pop the trunk."

By the time that Dexter had gotten out of the car, Helen was functioning as if she was in a mental fog. She began to fumble in her purse, looking for her cell phone. (Still Small Voice in Helen's Head: "You just lost a good guy." Loud Voice: "He just lost a great lady!!")

Dexter rapped on the trunk to let Helen know that he was clear of the car but never looked back at her as he walked away from the car. He then handed the skycap his ID. As Helen was about to drive off, she looked in the rearview mirror and noticed Dexter moving away from the car. Before proceeding, she checked her driver's side mirror and slowly merged into the airport traffic.

She thought, "At last!" She finally had a sense of relief, now that her marriage was finally over. She and Dexter had fun in the early years of their marriage, but over the years Helen had discovered that Dexter was a timid man, without much backbone. That was one of many unacceptable features that had become apparent to her. She wanted a confident man who would take control, who was a go-getter, and who would shower her with admiration. "She smiled and chuckled, saying to herself, "FRICKING loser!"

Dexter had his ticket validated, checked in his luggage, and got in line to board his plane. He thought to himself, "This trip came at a really good time. I can clear my head and I can get back to the basics of coaching…pick and roll on offense, blocking and spacing on defense. I can now put my game face on."

Helen may have thought of him as a loser, but Dexter was determined to prove her wrong. He believed that this upcoming season, with his new point guard whom he had already secretly named Lightning would be stellar for him. Dexter had high hopes for what Lightning would do for the team and for his future because the boy had moves that reminded Dexter of ones that the ole Hurricane used to do in New Orleans back in the day.

Dexter had gotten out of line and sat down until the line became a little shorter. He snapped back to attention when he heard his flight being called and got back in the boarding line.

Although he was leaving Houston and his marriage, he was regaining his life. The ending of his life with Helen was leading to a new beginning without her.

On the way home, Helen was visited by the voices in her head. (Loud Voice: "F@#K that LIL MAN. You deserve better." Still Small Voice: Silence.) Helen looked forward to getting home, taking a bubble bath, and reading a good book. She was also really looking forward to getting a break from her conscience.

She began to reflect back on her evening with Brandon. "Life is full of moments," Helen thought. "This is one moment that I want to savor." That evening, Brandon had shown her his new four-bedroom house with an outdoor swimming pool. The area around the pool was lit and there were two glasses of champagne sitting on the table when she arrived.

That evening, Brandon had treated Helen to a lovely dinner, the main course of which was baked salmon and asparagus, with orange duck sauce. He must have lit at least a hundred candles around the house. Their scent made the house smell wonderful.

Before going to Brandon's house, Helen had vowed that she would resist his charms if he tried anything. However, by the time that the evening had progressed, being intoxicated by both Brandon and the champagne, when he led her to his bedroom, Helen's feeble attempts to fight Brandon off failed miserably, as did her resolve to wait until she got to know him better. She really wanted him. She knew it and so did Brandon.

Yielding to the compulsion of her senses, Helen fell into Brandon's arms. They spent the remainder of the evening locked in each other's embrace, exchanging passionate kisses, and engaging in sensual explorations that transported Helen to an indescribable state of ecstasy.

Brandon turned out to be a wonderful lover. He was gentle, patient, attentive, and adventurous. Brandon had made Helen feel sensations that she had not experienced since she had her first sexual encounters in high school. Their tryst reminded Helen of a scene from the series Desperate Housewives, an instance in which forbiddance led to passion.

Helen had hoped that a relaxing bath would help free her mind from the voices in her head that had been agitating her. However, that did not happen. The voices resurfaced. (Still Small Voice: "You sinned and missed the mark!" Loud Voice: Yeah, but don't it feel good!?")

CHAPTER 15

CONSEQUENCES

Armani decided to drive the convertible Jaguar instead of the Mercedes, given that Helen would not be coming to Atlanta with Cane. He also thought that picking up Dexter in the Jaguar would be a good idea. He thought Dexter could probably use a little sun right about now to brighten up his life.

As Armani headed for the airport, the temperature was right at eighty degrees. Sporting his Ray-Ban sunglasses, Armani merged onto I-285 at 5: 30 p.m.—just in time for a rush hour or Atlanta's game of vehicle ping-pong. The driving time to the airport was only thirty minutes, but with traffic, based on Armani's calculations, he would be about fifteen minutes late in picking up his baby brother. It was okay with Armani because he did not plan to take Dexter straight home. Instead, he had told Martina to bring Anna Marie or one of the other waitresses, and join them for happy hour at Tropical Ice.

Armani was excited about seeing Cane. It had been a while since he had seen him. Armani had always loved his brother, but he and Dexter had not always been as close as they were now. Dexter shared many of the details of his life with him now, Armani now felt like his Big brother. Dexter felt that he had only Armani to turn to for a sympathetic ear, guidance, and consolation. He and his brother had now become brothers for real.

Dexter had always wished that he had been able to share the events in his life with Helen. Lately, though only sharing they did was related to bills. Helen had never been interested in what he was feeling or going through especially concerning coaching. And now, with the divorce proceedings looming, Dexter felt he had the right to remain silent. That left him with Armani to try to fill the void.

He did not realize it, but often when they were speaking on the telephone—even though Armani was listening to Dexter—Armani was really working on one of his accounts in his head. Armani would just periodically say, with animation, "hmm uh" or "WOW!" in order to keep the conversations going.

Armani's occasional inattentiveness when Dexter was speaking was not an indication that he did not love Dexter. He did. When the sports spotlight was on him hard, Armani knew that he could always count on Cane to watch his back. With all of the ladies, press people, sports agents, and booster club personnel trying to coattail him, he needed someone he could trust. His mom and his baby brother were his rock during those years.

Armani made another weave through traffic. He deftly zipped into the middle lane of the highway in order to avoid getting caught in stopped traffic. This snarl was caused by a rubbernecker who was looking at the police car with its blue lights flashing on the right shoulder of the interstate.

Armani pulled his cell phone out of the dashboard cubby hole and called Martina again. Once again, the call was sent to the voicemail. He placed the cell phone back into its hidden pouch and adjusted the radio control to a sports program. Armani could not wait until football season started in September. For him, that was when life began each year. He had season tickets for the Atlanta Falcons but rather than watch the games from the stands, he usually tried to watch from the field. How successful he was in getting onto the field depended on who was at the gate and on whether the gate keepers were fans from his playing days at Tech.

Dexter walked rapidly past the people exiting the train in the Atlanta airport. He had been in the airport before, and knew his way to the baggage claim area. He did not have that indecisive gait of most of the first-time visitors to the city. As he took the long escalator up, he had a sense of calm about Helen and himself and about their marriage breaking up. Then he thought, "My big bro got me a date and I'm in the ATL for the whole weekend…at the Ritz-Carlton…in Buckhead. It doesn't get any better than this!"

Dexter entered the baggage claim area and wondered if Armani was parked or riding around, as he usually did. Then he thought, "Knowing Mani, he's riding around trying not to pay to park." Dexter did not get it and thought, "Here this guy is quite well off but he hates to pay for parking." Shaking his head, he thought, "Rich people?! I guess that's how they stay rich?!"

Watching the luggage carousel, he spotted his flat bag and his suitcase, slid between two fat guys and scooped up both pieces, then headed for the airport exit to wait outside for Armani. When there was no sight of Armani he put on his "I'm waiting Helen again look." Then he noticed, however, that there were a lot fine sisters in Atlanta in comparison with Texas. Houston had beautiful women but they could not hold a candle to the number of beautiful, black professional women that you could find in the Atlanta area.

Armani, looking at the people waiting for transportation, scanned through the crowed to see if Dexter had found his luggage and had come outside. Driving slowly along the south curb, he found a smiling and waving Dexter. As Armani got closer, he heard the compliments that Dexter was shouting to him about his new Jaguar convertible.

Armani's elegant car was black with bronze leather seats. It had expensive rims that Armani had custom ordered. It also had chrome moldings on the sides and door panels. The car was so pimped-out, Dexter easily spotted it before he saw his brother.

Armani pulled up to the curb, stopped, and popped his trunk using the release button on the floor. Jumping out of the car, Armani shouted, "What up, Cane?" With them both smiling broadly, they hug each other like old friends. Dexter replied, "Looking good, big bro! Whoa dude!...I see you got the 'brains blown out!'" Armani looked puzzled as he pick-up Dexter's suit case. He looking to see if it could fit his diminished size trunk and asked, "What?!" Dexter explained, "You got the top dropped, bro. Get with it!"

Dexter had found that one of the many perks of working with children was being kept abreast of current slang. He thought being able to use it made him "hip."

However that did not work for Helen. She thought it made him look juvenile.

Dexter and Armani finished loading the luggage and jumped in the car. Armani had taken off his shades and put them in his breast pocket when he greeted Dexter. Ready to pull off, Armani whipped his shades, put them on, and slowly merged into traffic. To set the tone for the evening, he turned up the volume on the car radio so that they could better hear the smooth jazz that was now playing.

Armani wanted Cane to relax, enjoy the breeze, and let the rhythm of the music flow through him. "So how was your flight?" Armani asked, not wanting to start the conversation off with questions about the divorce. He wanted Dexter's trip to be about moving forward and not about looking back. Bobbing his head, Armani was now waiting for Martina to call and confirm the time of the planned happy hour.

Dexter was at peace. Right now everything was calm. There were no problems. He was feeling the vibe of the music, he was with his big brother, and he was enjoying the feeling of the cool breeze that was flowing over him. He was enjoying life again. The afternoon heat was a catharsis for his spirit. Tonight, Dexter he thought, "I want to feel as cool as the other side of the pillow."

Attempting to avoid the downtown Atlanta traffic, Armani skillfully maneuvered the Jaguar through the thick traffic like a running back exploding through an offensive line, heading towards the High Occupancy Vehicle (HOV) goal line. Finally, he heard the familiar sound caused by the vibration of his cell phone in the dashboard console. Looking over at Cane, Armani saw Dexter now bobbing his head too, and he smiled. Glancing at the phone, he answered and said, "Heeey, baby gurrrrlll. Talk to PAPI!!" He looked again at Cane, but he had been transported to la la land by the music and the wind blowing through his hair. Then Armani abruptly stopped talking, looked at his phone again, and screamed, "YOU ARE WHAT?!?"

Stunned by what Martina had said, Armani felt as if someone had put his life on freeze frame, like when a movie is advanced in slow motion. The parts of what Martina had said that he could remember were now popping in mind like flashes lights from the paparazzi.

Armani was so distracted by Martina's words that he completely forgot that he was driving on the interstate. He went blank momentarily, he did not see that the traffic had stopped. When he did come to himself, he remembered seeing the red Cyclops of the SUV in front of him. Then he his foot slipped off the brake.

Armani also vividly recalled the crunching sound that resulted when the Jaguar went under the SUV. His next flashbulb memory was his face recoiling back off the airbag that had deployed; but his last nightmare was when he looked over to passenger seat next to him to find it empty.

When he woke up, Armani learned that he was at Grady Memorial Hospital. He also learned that he and Dexter had been in a serious collision. Though he had been treated and was being discharged, Dexter was in critical condition and he was being kept in the hospital.

After Armani finished his discharge paperwork, he

went to the waiting room to wait for news about Dexter's condition. Armani stayed there until Shelia arrived to pick him up. She had been delayed after she had been informed about the accident because she had to take Sierra to a babysitter before coming to the hospital.

While waiting for Shelia, Armani tried to recall what had happened to Dexter. He remembered that when the collision occurred, Armani had had on his seat belt. However, Dexter was not wearing his. Therefore, when the air bag deployed on impact, Dexter was ejected from the car. Given that the highway traffic could not stop on a dime following the ejection, Dexter had been run over by two cars before anyone realized what had happened. When the ambulance arrived, the emergency technicians were able to keep him stabilized for a while, but by the time they arrived at the hospital, he had slipped into a coma.

Armani, holding his hand on the ice pack that he had been given for his neck, began going back in his mind to what event had triggered this whole mess. (Loud Voice in Armani's Head: "The Trick done got pregnant!" Still Small Voice: Silence.). While he was driving, Martina had told Armani that she was pregnant and Armani lost control of his vehicle.

Armani had been very careful when he and Martina had sex and, from the very beginning, he also had been candid with her about the nature of their relationship. He had made it very clear that he was not leaving his family. He had crafted an ideal image to go along with his profession, a beautiful white-wife and child was icing on the cake. Though Martina was beautiful and fascinating to him, she was a just piece on the side.

Moreover, although Armani was not being faithful to Shelia, he needed her. It had been quite some time since Armani had told Shelia of her significance to him. He knew that Shelia had always been an important partner in the making of his image. He also knew that her presence in his life was more important to his future than was any marketing idea that he could come up with. With her beauty, elegance, and grace, combined with his confident football player determination, they were a potent force. Armani had no intention of diluting that force.

Armani's mind was racing from one thing to another. Having brought his thoughts back to Dexter, Armani could simply not believe that his brother was in a coma and that the doctors had told him to get in contact with his next of kin. They did not think Dexter was going to make it. The guilt was overwhelming and was made worse by the accusing voice speaking in his head. (Loud Voice: "You killed Cane!" Still Small Voice: "It was an accident.")

Armani dropped his head in his hands, held his face, and began sobbing like a little child. He continued to cry, holding his face in his hands, until he felt the familiar hands of his wife on the small of his back. Her hands were massaging his back, rubbing it, using little circles. She rubbed the tense muscles in his back, moving in various directions, until she finally worked her fingers up to his shoulder blades.

Sympathetically, Shelia softly said, "It's okay, Pookie Poo!" Shelia repeatedly tried to comfort Armani, saying, "It's okay… It's okay." (Loud Voice in Armani's

Head: "You are cheating bastard! You don't deserve her!"
Still Small Voice: "See, you do need her.")

CHAPTER 16

TRUTH, REGRET, AND REVELATION

Helen became aware of the conversation going on between the voices in her head. (Loud Voice: "How WE going to bury this fool!" Still Small Voice: "It was an accident.") There was a flurry of questions and details in Helen's mind as she walked toward the Intensive Care Unit (ICU) of Grady Memorial Hospital.

Dexter had been in a coma and on life support for a full day and the doctors had told her that they doubted whether he could make it too much longer. Once she got the news, she called her mom for her credit card and took the next flight out of Houston to Atlanta. The news had shattered her whole Saturday…and her whole life.

Dexter's doctors had stopped his internal bleeding, but Dexter was still on a heart monitor, just in case he went into cardiac arrest again. Dexter was truly at death's door. Helen was thinking, "How could this happen to me, right before I am about to make it out clean, with a divorce?" So many thoughts were whirling around in her head, including the thought that she probably had made a mistake in not getting a bigger life insurance policy on Dexter just because they were splitting up.

Dexter may not have known it, but Helen had begun breaking up with him about a year ago, when she started making more money than he did. The split began when she saw him get too comfortable with her being the primary bread winner. When she realized that he was just fine with that scenario, she lost all respect for him. She knew that he was not even interested in trying to advance his career to college ranks. She summed him up as a loser.

Helen had a life insurance policy on herself through DHR. However, Dexter only had a $5,000.00 teacher's insurance policy. Helen had determined that his policy would probably only cover half of the funeral costs. After considering those expenses, she thought, "What about the house note, the car payments, and the lawn care contract that she had just signed a week ago?" Helen's mind was abuzz with disjointed thoughts as she entered the ICU waiting room, where she saw Armani sitting in a chair watching ESPN and Shelia talking on the phone, looking worried.

Helen's thoughts were racing. (Loud Voice in Helen's Head: "Ain't this a B%@CH! Here this fool is, kicking back." Still Small Voice: "It was an accident.") "Hey Armani," she blurted out as she waved to Shelia, still on the phone. Then she stopped in her tracks when she saw Dexter. She could not believe her eyes. Dexter was in a full body cast with his left leg elevated. His head was bandaged, but what got her attention most was that his head was twice its normal size. But what made her stop was the deep massive scar running from his nose to his forehead. It looked as if he had been dragged along the ground for some distance.

While she was trying to focus on the seriousness of Dexter's condition, Helen became aware of the distracting voices speaking in her head. (Loud Voice: "Damn. He's F@#KED UP!" Still Small Voice: Silence.) Helen had to look away to calm her nerves. Then she placed her purse on the table next to Dexter's bed, walked back out into the area where Shelia and Armani were sitting, and asked, "How's he doing?"

Armani, sitting up slightly, picked up the TV remote and started changing the channels. Then he burst out with the statement, "He's okay! He is going to be alright! The doctors don't know everything!" Hearing what Armani said and looking at him, Shelia ended her phone conversation. She had been calling the nurse to come in and look at one Dexter's bandages. She went over to Helen, gently gave her warm embrace, and whispered in her ear, "The Lord is sovereign. He's got this!"

Helen, looking a little puzzled at Shelia's statement, responded, "Hmmmmmmph." She frowned as she looked at Shelia. Her head cocked slightly to the right as she tried to quiet the agitated voices speaking in her head. (Loud Voice: "Let this B@#CH have it!!" Still Small Voice: Silence.)

Resisting the urge to cuss out Shelia, Helen turned her gaze, filled with pure evil, towards Armani, who was rocking lightly in the chair, and said, "So, Armani, tell me again what the F@#K happened!? Or, better yet, tell me the name of trick you're screwing. Tell me what she said to you to make you F@#K up my life like this!" Armani, rising up out of the chair as if his manhood had been insulted, shouted, "Look B@#CH, I done told you it was a client!" Shelia, placing herself between Helen and Armani, shouted firmly, "Enough! Enough!"

They were all startled by the light tap on the waiting room door, which was closed. When they looked towards the door, they saw the nurse enter forcefully. She said, "Look, I don't know where you people think you are, but you're in an ICU unit! For the sake of this patient—and of the other ones—you all need to take this feud outside!" They all looked like a deer caught in middle of the road on a dark night. From her tone of voice, they knew she meant business. Then they heard the heart monitor that was attached to Dexter begin to beep loudly and erratically. The nurse, Shelia, Armani, and Helen all turned towards Dexter's bed.

Next, to their bewilderment and disbelief, Dexter popped up in the bed. Still seated, he let out one of the most blood-curdling shrills that Armani had ever heard in his life. He began hollering at the top of his lungs: "HEEEEL-LLLP MEEEEE! HELLLLLLLLP ME! HELL IS REAL, HELL IS REAL! AAAUUGGUGG-UUGHHH …LISTEN TO THE STILL SMALL VOICE! AAAU-UGGGUGGGUGHH!" Then, he collapsed backwards in the bed; the heart monitor went silent and then a straight line appeared on the monitor's screen. The nurse rushed over to Dexter's bed and hit the red emergency button, frantically calling into the intercom on Dexter's bed, "CODE BLUE! WE HAVE A CODE BLUE!" Then she shouted to the three: "You have to leave!"

Medical personnel began flooding into Dexter's room. Armani, Shelia, and Helen were all were quickly escorted to waiting room, where they sat in stunned silence. Neither of them could fathom what had happened in Dexter's room, even though they all heard it with their own ears and saw it with their own eyes. The emptiness of the waiting room only magnified the silence.

Shelia, finally coming out of her fog, picked up her cell phone to call and check on Sierra. Armani then got up to go outside for some air. Helen just sat in the chair thinking and looking very afraid that her husband had just died. (Loud Voice in Helen's Head: "F@#K! F@#K!!" Still Small Voice in Helen's Head: "I'm still here.")

Armani walked towards the exit. He felt as though he could not breathe. When he got outside, he took a deep breath and thought to himself, "This has truly not happening to me!" He began thinking over everything that had happened in a few short hours. Between Dexter and Martina, his world had been turned completely upside down.

Martina's stunning news had given Armani much more than just a headache; it had given him heartache. He could have dealt with the pregnancy news, but for him to have "flipped out" about it and to have caused an accident that might take his brother's life...he just could not forgive himself for that. Still in a stupor of disbelief, Armani shook his head and thought, "How could I be so stupid and lose it like I did?" His head was throbbing, not just from the injuries that he had sustained in the accident, but also from the persistence of the shouting voices in his head. (Loud Voice: "YOU ARE A F@#K UP! KILL YOUR SELF!" Still Small Voice: "I'm here.")

Armani, vigorously rubbing his head as if doing so would make all of the distressing events of the day disappear from his thoughts, had a flashback to the exclamation that Dexter had shouted from his hospital bed. His mind replayed the awful sounds of agony that Cane had made.

With painful detail, Armani recalled seeing the extreme distress on his brother's face and hearing the fear in Dexter's voice as he hollered out, "Hell is real. Listen to the Still Small Voice!"

Armani's thoughts drifted back to his and Dexter's childhood. He remembered hearing about Hell the few times that their mom had taken them to church. But he did not remember ever hearing anything about a Still Small Voice. Then he lifted up his head to the sky and pleaded, "Lord if you are real help ME!"

CHAPTER 17

HIT IT AND QUIT IT!

Brandon looked at his cell phone and, sure enough, it was Helen Lewis again, so he decided to let the call go to voicemail. He knew that, eventually, he would have to cut Helen from his "starting player's list" and place her on the "bench" with the rest of the "reserves." Brandon had two other women already on the bench and Helen was next in line.

The bench players got a call when—and only if—all else had failed on a Friday or a Saturday night, after the club was closing. Or when it was a rainy night and he did not feel like going out exploring. The bench players knew the rules: First, you get the call and you are either "with it" or you are "not." Second, two or more "not's" could get you kicked off the team, depending on how good your sex was.

Brandon and Helen had been having sex regularly for the past three months. During this time, he had penetrated, explored, and licked pretty much every part of her body. Now he was bored and found the voices in his head shouting at him. (Loud Voice: "HER COOCHIE AIN'T ALL THAT! THERE IS ALWAYS SOMETHING BETTER!") "Variety is the spice of life…" he thought out loud.

Brandon stood in front of the full-length mirror that he had brought from his old office to his new one and adjusted his tie. While tightening the knot, he became distracted by the loquacious voices in his head. (Loud Voice: "Morris Chestnut! Morris Chestnut!") With his goatee coming in, he could definitely see the Morris Chestnut resemblance that women kept alluding to. Then he chuckled and thought, "Little Ms. Holy Ghost Girl Helen had turned out to be a big freak in the bed." What seemed really ironic to Brandon was that she got wilder after she left church.

Hanging with Helen had been fun. The sex had been good with her he reflected. But since her husband's death, she had become whiny, needy, and clingy. The fun had gone out their relationship. Now, all she did was complain about her bills and about how her husband's death had taken a serious toll on her finances.

Brandon sympathized with Helen's position, but he did not feel that, just because he was getting orgasms from her, he should be expected to pay her bills like a trick. When Brandon was with her, all he heard was: "My grass needs cutting"; "My car was on 'E' when I came over here"; "Why we can't go out!?..." Brandon ignored complaints and nodded, saying, "Uh Huh!"

Being fed up with Helen's crabbiness anyway, Brandon had found a new incentive to bench her. He was on to a new conquest, Ramona, whom he had met a few days earlier in the gym. He knew that he needed to sideline Helen so that he could devote his full energy to pursuing Ramona.

Brandon checked his calendar to see exactly what day he could give Helen the "You know what? This relationship is just not working" speech. He knew the routine well. He would take her to lunch and then pick a fight about a something small. Things like: "You have an odor"; "I didn't know you snore"; or "Why do you always smack when you eat?" Next, he would make a statement such as, "Anyway, you know, I've been thinking…this relationship really is not working out. Maybe we could be friends?"

After making a scene with Helen in the restaurant, Brandon planned to go into hiding in order to allow her time to reflect on why she made him go off on her. After he had completed planning how he would execute his breakup he chuckled and thought, "Women are such suckers for making-up sex. I can see how this will end: Helen will call me; I'll will say you made me go off! She will say How? Then I will say I got dinner for us, come over and let's talk!"

Visualizing the end of his Helen phase, Brandon threw his hands up in the air to simulate dunking a ball into a basketball hoop and shouted, "BAM! SWOOSHHH! Game over!" Then his thoughts began to wander to Ramona. (Loud Voice in Brandon's Head: "Imagine 'stroking' Ramona in the gym locker room!")

*****

A few days later

Helen was physically at work, but her mind was far away from her job. She had to make some decisions in a hurry because her new car was being repossessed. "If only Armani, with his rich, cheap A*S would have paid the balance of my new car, as I requested at the funeral," she thought.

Armani was horrified at Helen's timing and thought that she had been very rude to bring up the subject of her bills at Dexter's funeral. When Helen mentioned the subject, she and Armani got into an argument so heated that once again, Shelia had to place herself between the two of them to keep things from becoming really ugly. Being so angry with Armani, Helen packed her bags immediately after the funeral and took a taxi to airport to catch a flight back to Houston.

Later that night, Shelia called to check on her. She then informed her that she would make sure that Armani paid for the funeral. This freed Helen to use the insurance money to pay other debts. Delighted at Shelia's good news, she said, "You know what, for white girl, you're alright!"

Between paying the house note, the grass upkeep costs, her student loan and credit cards obligations, Helen's car note got behind. She had come to her wit's end. And to top the distress resulting from her financial woes, she had finally concluded that Mr. Wonderful was Mr. Full-of-SH*T!

She thought, "Dating is F@#KED up out here! You sex them down and, when they're done, they leave you! If you don't give 'em some, they leave you! What do these fools want? I'm tired of chasing Brandon Wilkes down… and besides, he really wasn't that much bigger than Dexter…Here he's been giving me the impression that he wanted me to move in with him and the whole time, he's just been using me as a booty call. At first he was calling me during the day and texting me at night…Lunches, dinner, and countless walks through the park. As soon as I give in to that turkey, he goes incog-negro!"

In the midst of her solitary tirade, a strange feeling came over Helen. It was the feeling that one might get when listening to the eerie music in a horror film. Her mind flashed to Dexter's face and she felt as though she was being haunted by Cane, from the grave. She kept hearing Dexter yelling, "Hell is real! Listen to the Still Small Voice!!"

Shaking herself, Helen rubbed her head, trying to quiet the voices yelling in her mind. (Loud Voice: "He was drugged up. Hell doesn't exist!" Still Small Voice. "Yes, it does!") She was still amazed by the fact that Dexter had actually popped up, like the lid of a trash can when you press the foot control, and shouted such blood-curdling sounds.

Helen understood the concept of Hell and she knew that if it existed, it was not a place that she wanted to go. Then she thought, "Hell doesn't exist. That's crazy." She reasoned to herself, "How could a good God even consider tormenting anyone?" (Loud Voice in Helen's Head: "GOD doesn't exist!" Still Small Voice: "JUDGEMENT DAY IS REAL!") Lost in thought, Helen wondered, "But...what of this Still Small Voice?"

Helen's office telephone rang, bringing her back to reality. "Ms Lewis," she answered, after picking up the phone. Recognizing the voice on the phone, she said, "Oh really?...And so now you need to see me?!...Uh huh!...Well, that might be okay, Mr. Wilkes." In response to Brandon's question about a good time for lunch, Helen responded, "Tomorrow is okay!...Jason's at noon?!...Oh really?!...Okay. See you then!"

Helen hung up the phone and let herself become excited, feeling that at least something was looking up for her today. She was now looking forward to her "boo" taking her to lunch tomorrow. Then she thought, "Maybe I could wear something enticing enough to get my nails done, or to get him to pay for my grass being cut, or to get something."

*****

The next day

Today was Friday, so Helen settled on a form-fitting, linen sundress that would give Mr. Wilkes a good view of the booty he had to have been missing by now. Brandon was sitting with his back towards the wall, in the corner of the bistro. When he saw Helen, he waved at her from across the restaurant. Spotting him, Helen thought to herself, "He used to stand in the foyer and escort me to my chair. Why can't men focus on the little things in a relationship?" Having already ordered, Brandon said, "Here's the menu." Next, he looked at his watch and said, "I've only got an hour today."

Helen was a bit offended and taken aback by the rapid firing of statements from Brandon. She adjusted her dress and sat in the booth. Taking the menu from Brandon, she asked, "And how are you, Mr. Wilkes?" Gasping for air as if he was caught off guard, Brandon hurriedly replied, "I'm cool, I'm cool! I've just been busy, girl. You know this new job got me going and coming."

Helen, perusing the menu, replied, "Yeah, I know. That's all I have been hearing from you lately, about this new job. What I can't figure out, Mr. Wilkes, is why—all of a sudden—I can't even get a return text?" Brandon, frowning, answered, "Look, this is a very demanding position for a black man. I got to stay on top of these white boys!" Brandon looked down and tuned in to the voices that were conversing in his head. (Loud Voice: "Dismiss this B@#CH!.") Then he stated firmly, "You know what, B@#TCH? I'm outta here!" He stood up and slammed the menu on the table. Shouting and waving his arms in the air, he said, "You know what!! I can't take this SH*T! No-mo! YOU DON'T HAVE A CLUE, TO THE PRESSURE I'M UNDER!"

Helen's mouth was hanging open during Brandon's unprovoked rant. She was leaning back in her chair, staring at him in total disbelief at the scene he was making over her request for an occasional text. Then, slamming his napkin down on the table, Brandon continued his tirade, stating bluntly, "This relationship is not working for me and be-sides…you have an odor! You may want to get checked out!" With those words, he quickly stood up and turned and stormed out of the restaurant.

Helen sat in stunned silence. She noticed that, seem-ingly, everyone in the restaurant was looking at her because of Brandon's explosive conduct. She picked up her cell phone and fumbled with it, as if she were checking for a text message, giving everyone in the room a chance to breathe again.

After several minutes had passed, Helen became aware that the volume of the voices in the restaurant had begun to rise to a more normal level. After she had determined that things had pretty much settled back to normal, she looked up and blankly stared around the room, not having the slightest clue about what to do. Finally, it seemed that no one was paying her much attention anymore. Then she breathed heavily and thought, "This may be a good time to try to make graceful exit." While trying to decide whether to go or stay, Helen thought back on something Brandon had said and thought, "A body odor? What a Body odor?! NOW he has a problem with my body odor? "

Rather than run out in dishonor, Helen decided to stay at Jason's. She ordered lunch and several glasses of wine. She ate quietly, somberly reflecting on life and on some of the bad choices that she had recently made. During her meal, she stopped eating and thought, "My life sucks!" In the midst of her epiphany, she became aware that she had a throbbing headache, which was not being helped by the wine she had been drinking or by the deafening voices yelling in her head. (Loud Voice: "Kill yourself FOOL!" Still Small Voice: "PEACE BE STILL!")

Helen now considered her social life and her finances. Her life had been thrown into a tailspin and she did not know what area of her life she should address first. Though she recognized that she needed to make several life changes, the main question that kept nagging her was what to make of the Still Small Voice she kept hearing, it was now a comfort.

*****

As Brandon entered his condo-style office building, he looked at his watch and thought, "Wonder what Ramona is wearing today?!" Then thinking of the restaurant scene with Helen, Brandon began to smile slightly, thinking, "It went as well as I could've expected. Helen will be stunned for a few days and then she will call, requesting an explanation, but I won't answer any calls for at least a couple of weeks."

Brandon's thoughts drifted away from Helen and returned to Ramona. He could not seem to shake her from his thoughts for some reason. He kept hearing a voice in his mind urging him to call her. (Loud Voice: "Call for Ramona!") Seemingly unable to resist his desire to contact the new object of his obsession, Brandon picked up his cell phone, flipped it open, and dialed directory assistance to get the number to the gym where he and Ramona worked out.

Brandon had gotten Ramona's name from a girl at the gym who had been working out near her one day. On one occasion, Brandon had noticed that Ramona was wearing a name badge and he wondered if the guy manning the front desk of the gym had noticed the name of the company where she worked. As he dialed the telephone number of the gym, Brandon thought, "Ah, the hunt is on! The chase is truly the fun part." (Loud Voice in Brandon's Head: "Ain't nobody bad like you, BOY!!")

CHAPTER 18

SEEING THE LIGHT

3 months later

Armani opened his eyes and looked at the clock. It was exactly 3:00 a.m. AGAIN. Something had been waking him up at exactly this time every morning for the past two weeks. He thought he was suffering from a guilty conscience because he had caused Cane's death. But this time, the feeling he had was different, it was weird.

Frustrated, he got up and went into the bathroom to wash his face. Next, he began to shudder, as if the room had suddenly become cold. Then, just as abruptly, an intense sense of peace came over him and he felt a familiar, yet unfamiliar presence within his heart. After experiencing the unknown presence, Armani heard a voice that seemed so nearly audible, he thought someone else was in the room. The voice said, "YOU ARE MY SON!!" Suddenly, Armani felt so overwhelmed with joy that tears began streaming down his face and he began to cry, mightily. After crying for a few minutes, Armani heard a Still Small Voice say to his heart: "YOU ARE MY SON!"

Armani had heard voices in his head before, but they had never been so clear to him. As he thought about the words he felt as if this moment had happened in his life before. Armani was immediately reminded of the words that Cane spoke when he popped up in his hospital bed and said, "Listen to the Still Small Voice."

(Still Small Voice in Armani's Head: "YOU ARE MY SON!"). Armani recognized that this was the voice to which Dexter had been referring on his death bed. Armani began saying in his heart, and then out loud, "God, I thank you. Lord, I thank you!"

Though his thoughts had slowed, when he heard the voice of the Lord, Armani had never stopped crying. He began to cry, all the more, when he recognized the voice of the Lord as the Still Small Voice. Tears cascaded down his face. He cried so heavily that, seemingly, there were enough tears to fill a bucket.

Armani felt completely spent when he felt the well-known hands of his wife. Feeling his energy renewed by Shelia's touch, Armani gently pulled her hand, urging her to join him on the floor. Shelia did so and they both knelt on the side of their bed. Shelia began saying, "Jesus! Jesus! Jesus! Yes, Lord…Yes, Jesus…We hear You, Lord…Yes, Jesus." They both honored the Lord with praise and cried in each other's arms until daybreak. Finally, about 8:00, Armani called his assistant and cancelled his appointments for the day. Shelia had called in too. She was now in the kitchen cooking breakfast.

After his experience during the night, Armani knew that he had to sort out some things that he was feeling in his heart and mind. He knew that TODAY was the day that he needed to make some decisions about his life. He thought, "To whom shall I listen? The Loud Voice that was negative or the Still Small Voice that was encouraging and positive." Armani was in deep thought, as he heard a voice speak:

"YOU ARE MY SON!" He then felt at peace.

After Armani called in to report that he would not be in that day, he reflected over the events. Armani realized that something had happened to him but he was not sure exactly what. Deep in thought, he asked, "Lord! What will you have me to do?" Then he heard the Still Small Voice of the Lord speak clearly: "Feed my sheep!" He did not immediately know what the Word from the Lord meant, because he was stretched out on the floor sobbing. He decided to hide this encounter in his heart and would wait for further guidance.

Having received some peace after receiving a word from the Lord, Armani's tranquility was disrupted by the ringing of his cell phone. When he got up to look to at the phone, he noticed it was Martina was calling. He decided to let the call go to the voicemail. Armani did not know why, but he knew that right now, he was not able to speak with Martina—or with anyone else—while he was still dealing with the changes that had begun to occur in his spirit.

Shelia had entered the room expecting to find her husband on his treadmill, but instead she found a disheveled mess sitting on the edge of the chaise lounge with his head held down. Armani was unshaven, was wearing a t-shirt and boxers, and looked as if he were mentally in outer space. Though he looked like a mess, Shelia was smiling and she looked up and mouthed silently, "Thank you, Lord!" She could not have been happier in her entire life. She had been praying for this moment for her husband since it had happened to her at church. Armani may not have known what happened, but she did. Armani had just been "born again." Smiling, Shelia approached Armani and offered him a cup of coffee.

Hearing Shelia enter the room, Armani looked up with a smile, and extended his right hand to receive the coffee mug that she was handing him. He said, "Thanks, babe." Shelia, sitting on the edge of the bed across from him on the lounger, politely asked, "You okay, Pookie Poo!?"

Armani, looking slightly puzzled, replied, "Yeah. I'm okay…I guess…so what just happened to me?" Shelia replied, "You answered your phone." Armani, thinking she heard his cell phone ring, responded, "No I didn't." Shelia smiled, knowing that Armani did not have a clue which phone she was talking about, said, "YES, YOU DID. You answered the phone in your heart." Armani, frowning, asked, "Huh? What phone?"

Shelia leaned closer to Armani and explained, "When we are born, God places two phones in our heart. They both speak to us about decisions we make in life. One phone is the Loud Phone, or the voice of Satan that leads to death and destruction. The second phone is the Still Small Voice of God that leads to life eternal." After explaining the spiritual phone system to Armani, Shelia said. "Baby, God speaks in quiet ways so you have to concentrate on your inner thoughts and, sometimes, it is only when we stop and keep silent that God can really get through to us. God made you stop and pick up your silent voice phone."

Following Shelia's explanation, Armani had gained some understanding of what had happened to him during the night. However, still trying to make some sense of all the information that he had received, he asked Shelia, "So I have two voices in my head." Shelia responded yes. She then said, "When Cane shouted out, 'Listen to the Still Small Voice,' he was giving you the key to escape the damnation fires in Hell." Armani then sat up in his chair.

Trying to get fuller meaning of it all, he asked, "So now what do I do?" Shelia smiled, got up, and retrieved the Bible from her night stand. She handed it to Armani and said, "Get to work, buddy...We have a lot of work to do!" Armani accepted the Bible, placed it on his lap, and said, "WE?" Shelia now half laughing said, "Yes, WE...you, me, and the Holy Spirit."

For Armani, the mystery of his spiritual development had just expanded. He looked at Shelia, with a puzzled look, and asked, "The Holy Spirit?" Shelia responded, "Yes! The Holy Spirit is the one who took your hand and made you answer the phone." Shelia ended her explanation by pointing to the Bible and saying, "Now you have ears to hear."

Armani, trying to make light of the situation because it was getting way too heavy for him, said, "It's like that the TV Commercial that asks, 'Can you hear me now?'" Shelia laughed, nodded her head, and said, "Exactly, Pookie Poo!" Then she leaned in and kissed his forehead and placed his head on her chest.

With Shelia's help, Armani had begun to realize the gravity of the information that he just received. However, for the moment, he had one more question and asked, "So everyone that doesn't listen to the Still Small Voice ends up where Cane is?" Shelia, rubbing the back of his neck, said,

"That's right, baby. It's a sad fact but that's the truth."

*****

In another part of town

Martina slammed the phone down. Every time she called Armani now, her calls were going to the voicemail. But today, apparently, he now had his phone turned off. She was furious with him for not taking her calls since his brother had died. She had left him numerous voicemail messages and texts saying how sorry she was. Though she understood why Armani was angry with her about the pregnancy, she did not think that it was right for him to blame her for the death of his brother. After all, she was not driving the car and she did not tell that fool not to wear his seat belt.

According to Martina's plan, Armani would begin divorce proceedings if he thought that she was having his child. After everything had gone so dreadfully wrong, she realized that she had told a horrible lie. She thought that their baby would be the little push that Armani needed to leave his family and come after her. Anna Marie had tried to talk her out of her little scheme, but she would not listen. Instead, she thought, "She doesn't know SH*T!"

The phone call she made to Armani on the day of the collision was supposed to be the call that started her life on a new course. She got a new beginning, but not the one that she had imagined. In fact, her plan had failed wretchedly. With one stupid action, she lost her Mani, her way out of her hell-hole of a job, and the one bed-room apartment she was living in.

As she reflected over the situation with Armani, Martina asked herself, "How could this have gone so wrong?" She wouldn't be surprised if Armani never spoke to her again. This did not stop her from thinking about him or from wanting to see him. (Loud Voice in Martina's Head: "Call his job!") While she was trying to decide whether to call Armani again, Martina heard the voices speaking in her head. However, the only voice that she wanted to hear was the one that encouraged her to try again to reach Armani.

Encouragement to persevere was exactly what Martina wanted right now. She thought to herself, "We could've been so great together! He's smart, rich, and handsome and I'm beautiful. I deserve to be happy and to live in a house like the one that I saw in that magazine."

CHAPTER 19

GOD'S AMAZING GRACE

"Lord, help me!" Helen silently prayed as she was being shown back to the waiting room in her doctor's office. Distressed by not knowing what was going on with herself, she heard all kind of voices shouting in her head as she was walking to the waiting room. (Still Small Voice: "I am with you!" Loud Voice: "You are going to die!")

It was ironic that Brandon had told Helen to get herself checked. The foul odor that he had mentioned turned out to be the result of gonorrhea, which he had given her. She shook her head, feeling stupid that she could have fallen for Brandon so easily. As Helen was being escorted to the doctor's office to receive a penicillin shot, she looked at her watch, hoping that the treatment would not take too long because she had to be back at the office for a meeting by 1:30 p.m.

Helen was at low point in her life. Now, there's the waiting. The doctors told her that it would be another day before she would receive the results of her HIV test. Her new car had been repossessed and the student loan agencies were constantly harassing her so much that she had begun screening her calls. To top that off, the condition of her yard made her the laughing stock of her community.

After reaching the examination room, a young nursing assistant politely said to Helen, "Please sit here, ma'am. The doctor will be with you shortly." Helen nodded and placed her purse and cell phone on the table next to the examination table. Then she sat down on the table, feeling angry because she felt that Brandon was being a total butt about the whole situation. He never even returned her calls or texts even after she left him a voice message informing him that he had given her a disease.

Seeking a distraction, Helen found herself thinking, "My payment on my Macy's card is due Tuesday." Then, swiftly, an intense sense of peace came over her and she felt a familiar, yet unfamiliar, presence within her heart. Next, Helen heard a voice that was so audible, she thought someone else was in the room. The voice said, "YOU ARE MY CHILD!" Tears started streaming down her face and she cried loud and hard.

After she had been crying for some time, within herself, Helen heard a voice speaking. (Still Small Voice: "You are my child!"). She had never heard the voice speak so loudly before. Next, the voice said something that reminded her of words that Cane spoke on his death bed. (Still Small Voice: "Peace BE STILL!!") Helen now realized that the Still Small Voice that Dexter referred to was the voice of the Lord.

Having received a revelation of the Spirit of God, Helen was overcome with emotion and got down off the exam table and onto her knees. She started shouting, "Thank You, Jesus! Thank you Lord! Thank You Jesus!" She was yelling so loudly, the nursing assistant and the doctor rushed into the room to see what the problem was. Seeing Helen on the floor, on her knees, the doctor and his assistant rushed over to her to extend their hands to help her get up and back on the exam table. Almost in unison, they asked," Are you okay, Miss?"

While on her knees, Helen had fallen back against the side of the examination table, and had gone totally limp. When she heard the voices of the doctor and nursing assistant calling to her, she came back to reality and replied, "Yes. Yes, I'm fine. Thank you." Grasping the hands of the doctor who pulled her up, she repeated, "Thank you! Jesus!" and asked, "May I have some water, please?" The doctor nodded and his assistant exited the room to get some water. (Still Small Voice in Helen's Head: "I am with you!") Looking at Helen with a puzzled expression, the doctor asked, "Are you sure you are okay?" Helen, smiling, replied, "I'm beyond okay. I'm blessed!"

About to begin Helen's treatment, the doctor heard a noise coming from behind him, and looked in the direction of the sound. Looking towards the table next to the examination table, he saw Helen's cell phone jumping and realized that the phone must have been set to vibrate. Looking at Helen, as if to seek her permission to check the phone, the doctor picked up the phone, looked at the screen, and told her that the "Shelia" was caslling. Then he asked Helen if she needed to take the call. Helen froze for a moment, having become distracted by the conflicting voices speaking in her head. (Still Small Voice: "Take the call!") Smiling, Helen replied, "Yes, doctor, Thank you. Can you give me a minute?"

*****

In another part of town

Brandon Wilkes leaned back in his chair so that he could look at himself in the mirror while he was talking on the phone. (Loud Voice in Brandon's head: "Boy, you're smooth!") Speaking into his office telephone, he said, "Yeah. I saw you on the treadmill when I first came in the gym!" "Oh really?" Ramona asked, appearing to be mildly surprised by Brandon's interest. "Yeah. I had to do some serious searching to find out where you worked." Ramona responded, "Hmmm huh." Brandon continued, "I just wanted you to know that I find you very attractive and I wanted to know if I could take you to lunch sometime?" Then Brandon sat up in his chair and exclaimed, "Oh, so you are married!"

CHAPTER 20

THE JUDGMENT

Many years later

"JESUS IS LORD!" Brandon stated loudly, arising after kneeling. He stood crying and trembling before Jesus Christ, the Lord. "BRANDON ADONIS WILKES!" thundered the Voice of the Lord God. "SEARCH THE BOOK OF LIFE," He Who Reigns commanded.

The Book of Life automatically opened. Then an angel said, "Lord, he is measured and is found wanting!" Following the angel's report, the atmosphere was filled with the sound of gasps uttered by the Heavenly hosts and silence enveloped the Great White Throne of the Lord of Hosts, in the same way that a drape would completely cover a chair. Jesus, the King of Kings, compassionately asked, "BRANDON, BRANDON. Why did you reject me?

Brandon raised his head and shouted, "Reject you? Reject You? When did I reject you?"

The Lord of Lords thundered, "SHOW THE EVIDENCE!" First, God revealed to Brandon a time in his life when he was fifteen years old and he was attending a church revival with a girlfriend. Next, God showed Brandon the church's pastor extending an invitation for him to come to the altar. The Lord Jesus likened the pastor's invitation, made with open hands and open arms, to the invitation made by Himself to humanity from the Cross. God told

Brandon, "Through the pastor's invitation, at that service, I was literally begging you to come to me. However, rather than to accept the altar call and to submit to my Still Small Voice, which resided in your heart, you chose to listen to the Loud Voice that spoke into your spirit, which urged you to 'Wait. Do it later.'"

In making His case that Brandon had rejected Him, God, the Wonderful Counselor, presented to Brandon a second evidentiary exhibit. God stated to Brandon, "This exhibit reveals an incident that occurred on a night on which you had gotten drunk after having listened to the Loud Voice that spoke into your spirit. God reminded Brandon that he had been in a room in which there was a gun and that the Loud Voice had told him to kill himself. God revealed to Brandon, "It was my Still Small Voice that saved your life by speaking into your spirit and by admonishing you not to harm yourself and to get up and go home."

Brandon began gnashing his teeth and crying. Feeling downcast, he heard a familiar loud voice in his soul: "F@#K THIS SH@#T!" After that tirade, God the Father, the Joy to the World, presented to Brandon a final evidentiary exhibit. God stated to Brandon, "This exhibit reveals a time when you had been driving and a certain gospel song came on the radio. As the song played, my Still Small Voice said to you, 'Listen to THIS!' To counter my directions, the Loud Voice urged you to change the radio station and you did."

Brandon held his head down and started wailing. Tears flowed like flood waters down Brandon's face, and he became aware of a voice speaking inside him: "F@#K

THIS SH@#T! F@#K GOD!" Next, Brandon bent over and screamed in an evil, shrill voice: "F@#k this SH@#$! F@#K You, God!" Following his outburst, he was instantly transported away from light of the Lamb's Throne and was cast out of Heaven into utter Darkness.

"Martina Alma Alvarez! Come out!" ordered the Holy Lamb of God. Immediately, Martina was ushered into the presence of the Lord. His voice thundered out the question, "IS HER NAME IN THE BOOK OF LIFE?" The Book of Life automatically opened and an angel said, "Lord, she is measured and is found wanting!" Martina lay prostrate before God; then she rose to her knees and shouted, "JESUS IS LORD!"

The Lord God stood up, took Martina by her hands, pulled her up to her feet, and lovingly said, "TINA, TINA. Why did you say no to me when you saw me?" Martina, not looking at God, heard a loud voice in her heart saying, "F@#K THIS! F@#K GOD!" Then she heard herself scream, "F@#K$ THIS SH@#T! WHEN DID I EVER F@#$KING SEE YOU!?" In response to her outburst, the Lord did not cast her out of His presence. Instead, He thundered, "SHOW THE EVIDENCE!"

God revealed to Martina a time in her life when she was lying in a field looking up at the sky at the age of seven years old. He reminded Martina that, as she lay in the field, her eyes were closed and she was reflecting on the image that He had revealed to her. God also reminded Martina that her peaceful image was interrupted by the Loud Voice in her head that shouted to her the question, "What if there was no GOD?" He also reminded her that He, by His Still

Small Voice, spoke into Martina's spirit and answered the question of the Loud Voice, stating, "There would be nothing forever and ever!" Finally, God reminded Martina that, after hearing His Still Small Voice," she got up from her field rest, having realized that her own existence and the existence of the universe were proof that, surely, there was a God.

The Lord GOD said to Martina, "You heard my Still Small Voice. However, you did not hearken unto my voice, even though I personally taught you of my existence." After presenting His evidence to Martina, the Lord God lovingly said to her, "Sadly, I never knew you. Depart from me, you worker of iniquity." Martina started wailing out loud and gnashing her teeth in agony and regret. With sorrow, God commanded that she be cast out of Heaven, instantly, into utter Darkness.

*****

In another part of Hell

"UGGGH EEE YYOOOWWW!" was the sound that Brandon repeatedly yelled as his soul experienced intense pain caused by the tormenting fires of Hell. Four hundred years after having been cast out of God's presence, into the darkness, Brandon was exhausted. Despite the passage of time and the pain and misery caused by the heat and intensity of Hell's fires, they had not at all diminished. Even after all this time, they were exactly as they had been when he first arrived in Hell.

During his time in Hell, Brandon had an opportunity to reflect on his life and on many spiritual issues, including the majesty of Heaven, the error of his ways, the mistake that he made in running away from Christ, and the benefits of avoiding Hell.

During the four hundred years of his banishment to Hell, Brandon had experienced many of the innumerable reasons to avoid Hell. The worst were the excruciating pains and torments inflicted upon his soul. The tormenting pain never relented and came in powerful waves, ranging from crazy to dreadfully insane.

For Brandon, the indescribable pain inflicted by the fires and demons of Hell was bad enough. However, there were other horrors too. The horrendous smell in his pit where he lived was lethal. The odor was so foul, he perpetually wanted to retch. Also, there was the continual demonic torment. The demons assigned to torment him would cease, for awhile. The break from the torment was a cause for dread, however, not celebration, because he knew that the demons would return…they always did.

(Loud voice in Brandon's spirit: "F#$K F@#$! F#$K GOD!") A wave of intense pain hit Brandon again. "UGGGGH EEEE YYOOOOWWWW UUUUGGGGGGG MOMMA!!!!!!"The Loud Voice that had spoken into his spirit in life was with him, in Hell, for eternity! Now, every time the Loud Voice spoke into his spirit, he experienced pain so intense, he wanted to die, again, to get relief.

In Hell, Brandon had found himself in an awful state and he wondered why no one had warned him about the horrors of that place. In addition to all the other detrimental consequences, he was always afraid in Hell. Since there was no light in the pits of Hell, hideous demons would come up behind him, at any time, without warning, to torment him.

Brandon then scratched his throat because it was dry as it always was. That discomfort was worsened by the impact of the mental images that he recalled of the pleasure that he had experienced in life, such as drinking a tall glass of cold water on a hot day. There being no relief for him, the image of his thirst being quenched haunted him, like the unshakable effects of a bad movie.

Brandon had found one bright spot, if one could call it that, about being in Hell. He had gotten a chance to see that "B@#CH Boy" Satan, and he was glad that he had. He thought to himself, "You know what? Come to think of it Satan looks nothing like what I saw in the movies. This MOTHER turns out to be a frail, pea-green, grotesque, little creature, with long floppy ears!" Shaking his head, Brandon thought out loud, "Ain't this a B@#CTH?!"

Satan was ushered into his solitary, isolated chamber, located in the deepest part of Hell. At any given time, you would hear him yelling louder than anyone else. No one in Hell ever came across anyone else because each person had his own chamber. Not only did each occupant of Hell have his or her own private quarters, he or she also had his or her own private pain. In Hell, the amount of pain and suffering to be borne by an individual depended on how much of the Word of Christ a particular individual had heard—and ignored, without repentance—in life.

Demons had returned to Brandon's pit and had resumed tormenting him. "EEEEE-WWWWW!!!!! YYYYYYYIIIII UGGGGH EEEE YYOOOOWWWW UUUUGGGGGGG MOMMA!!!!!!" Brandon had stopped yelling for God two hundred years ago, but now he called for his Momma because he thought maybe she was with him in Hell. Then Brandon yelled as he was experiencing excruciating pain. He wondered, "What would have happened to my life if I had paid attention to that damn Still Small Voice? EEEE-WWW!!!!! YYYYYYYIIIII UGGGGH EEEE YYOOOOWWWW UUUUGGGGGGG! MOMMAAA!!!!! HELP MEEEEEEE!!!!!!"

CHAPTER 21

REDEMPTION AND GLORIFICATION

A wave of intense pleasure came over Shelia, Armani, and Helen. The Still Small Voice had summoned them to the lobby of the Grand Ballroom. As Shelia watched Armani and Helen, hovering together, arm in arm like lovers on their honeymoon, she was just bursting with joy. "This is hilarious," she thought. "The two of them could not stand each other on earth, but now, look at them. Here, in Heaven, you can't keep them away from each other!" Overjoyed, she thought, "The Word of God is true…it IS good for brothers to dwell together in unity." This was another pleasant benefit that Shelia had discovered in Heaven.

Shelia had also discovered that the reason that God's Word never died was because it was always on full display in Heaven. The redeemed of the Lord were always saying so through their obedience to the Word. Everyone was patient, kind, and gentle towards each other and demonstrations of love abounded in Heaven. Shelia reflected on all of the benefits of Heaven that she enjoyed. She concluded that her favorite pastime definitely was walking up to Apostle Paul, quoting her favorite scripture to him, and watching him just laugh!

Shelia, Armani, and Helen were waiting in the lobby of the Grand Ballroom for Christ to make a surprise presentation to them. Sierra and their other family members had not been summoned to the ballroom. While anxious to discover what surprise Jesus had for them, Shelia could think of nothing more wonderful than the many gifts that the Lord had already bestowed upon them. Shelia fondly reflected over how the Lord Jesus had been so gracious to His children, at the time of the Judgment Seat of Christ.

Before coming to Heaven, Shelia feared judgment and thought of it as a punishment process. However, since being in Heaven, Shelia learned that the Judgment Seat was like attending a joyous awards ceremony, rather than a somber sentencing hearing. There, the Lord handed out gifts to those whose service in the Kingdom had been both great and small. He seemed to take particular pleasure in showering gifts on those often looked upon, on earth, as being the least in the Kingdom, such as the childcare workers, ushers, parking lot attendants, and especially the janitors who cheerfully and faithfully served in His church. When Armani, Shelia, and Helen went before God's Judgment Seat, the Lord blessed each of them with a Crown of Glory.

The Lord blessed them with the Crown for the Kingdom work that they had sown in the Cane is Able Ministries, which Armani had started in honor of his deceased brother Cane. Armani thought the name for the ministry was particularly fitting, considering that it was Dexter, on his deathbed, who had given him a revelation of Hell and who had been the inspiration for him seeking, finding, and following the Still Small Voice of God.

The Cane Is Able (CIA) Ministries had gotten off to a slow start as Armani and Shelia sought the guidance of the Small Still Voice as to in which direction the ministry should go. As the plan of the ministry unfolded, Armani's diligent work ethic and perseverance proved invaluable. The Small Still Voice instructed him to target children and enabled him to fashion a successful marketing strategy that taught children how to be CIA agents for GOD.

There were numerous lessons that God placed in their spirits to teach the children. One lesson that the CIA Ministries taught the children was that everyone is born with two voices in their heart. A second lesson that the Ministries taught the children was how to recognize the voices, one of which was the Still Small Voice of God that would lead them to the knowledge of good. The other voice that the children were taught to recognize was the Loud Voice of Satan that would lead them to the knowledge of evil.

Shelia had become the perfect help meet for Armani, both in their marriage and in the Cane Is Able Ministries. She grew to love the ministry and was supportive of Armani's work with children. She was always so proud each time she observed him applying illustrations that he developed, based largely on his employment with the Lawson Advertising firm, to teach the children about the voices. For example, sometimes when Armani would walk into a room of children, he would exclaim, "God is looking for Tyrone to pick up his phone!"

A third lesson that the CIA Ministries taught the children was how to listen for and distinguish between the voice of God and the voice of Satan; how Satan uses the noisy distractions of music, TV shows, movies, and ungodly habits to drown out God's Still Small Voice in their spirits; and that the only way to hear God's Still Small Voice is to turn off the TV, the music, and any other distractions, and to go into a quiet room and meditate for seven minutes.

The number "seven" was not supernatural. Understanding that children, generally, had a short attention span, Armani chose a small amount of time, like seven minutes so that the children would not be dissuaded by the length of time from seeking quiet time with the Lord. Armani encouraged the children to seek the Lord at any time of the day, but he especially encouraged them to spend time with the Lord in the mornings, when distractions would likely be fewer.

A fourth lesson that the CIA Ministries taught the children was the long-term benefits of meditation in God's Word. Armani explained to the children that daily, undistracted time seeking God's presence and wisdom would position them to seek God's thoughts, which would lead them to seek God's Words. Taking this time would lead them to seek to develop and undertake God approved actions, which would allow them to seek and develop God approved habits, practices, and character, which ultimately would lead them to the reward of being at peace.

From the foundation of the world, God selected His "chosen." The children chosen from the foundation of the world took to the messages that Armani taught like bees took to pollen. Armani knew that he was carrying out the will of God when he observed his children demonstrating knowledge gained from the lessons that he had taught them.

His heart was truly blessed when the children, speaking to one another, would say things like, "What voice have you been listening to?" or "Have you picked up your still small phone?" Or even, "You must be talking through your Loud Voice!?"

Back in the ballroom lobby, waiting for the Lord to arrive, Helen, Shelia, and Armani hovered about, comparing their crowns. Each one was uniquely designed for the glorified bodies that they had received in Heaven.

Shelia loved Heaven. There were so many blessings that she experienced there, but she was particularly blessed to experience having the anointed relationship with her husband that had eluded them on earth. Also, Shelia found that she did not have to wander through Heaven as she had done in life before she met Christ. Before she met the Lord, she felt emptiness in her life. In life, she was always worried about what could happen. Half of her life, she was worrying about whether she was going to lose her job, if she was going to lose her house, or when she was going to die. But when Christ became her Lord, the Still Small Voice of God guided her on earth and she gave God praise that His VOICE was still guiding her, even in Heaven.

Shelia rejoiced in her spirit at her revelation of the truth that Jesus spoke when He said, "I will be with you always!" Even in Heaven, the Still Small Voice of God was an encouraging source of comfort that truly made her feel like a beloved member of the family of God. No earthly pleasure that Shelia could recall even came close to bringing her the feeling of ecstatic joy that she experienced each time that she heard the Voice of God speak in her spirit.

God's Voice brought the most intense pleasure, which was 7 million times better than any orgasm that she had ever experienced on earth.

An intense wave of joy came over Helen, Shelia and Armani as they heard the Still Small Voice exclaim, "LET THE DOOR BE OPENED!" When those words were spoken, the doors opened, slowly, and the three of them saw an image that caused them to gasp and stare, with their mouths open. There…behind the door…stood the glorified body of a person that they had once loved and he was wearing a Crown of Glory. With their arms outstretched, with immense joy, in unison, they shouted, "CANE! CANE! CANE!"

THE BEGINNING

CLOSING REFLECTION

"But Jesus beheld them, and said unto them, with men this is impossible; but with God all things are possible."
Matthew 19:26

And he said, Go forth, and stand upon the mount before the LORD. And, behold, the LORD passed by, and a great and strong wind rent the mountains,and brake in pieces the rocks before the LORD; but the LORD was not in the wind: and after the wind an earthquake; but the LORD was not in the earthquake: And after the earthquake a fire; but the LORD was not in the fire:and after the fire a still small voice.
1 Kings 19:11-12

Twaddel